REVENGE STREAK

DI SARA RAMSEY
BOOK TWENTY-TWO

M A COMLEY

For Mum, you never let me down, thank you for giving me the tools and the backing to begin this incredible journey.

Miss you every minute of every day, you truly were a Mum in a million. My heart, my soul.

ACKNOWLEDGMENTS

Special thanks as always go to @studioenp for their superb cover design expertise.

My heartfelt thanks go to my wonderful editor Emmy, and my proofreaders Joseph and Barbara for spotting all the lingering nits.

Thank you also to my amazing ARC Group who help to keep me sane during this process.

To Mary, gone, but never forgotten. I hope you found the peace you were searching for my dear friend. I miss you each and every day.

ALSO BY M A COMLEY

Murder by the Sea

Death on the Coast

Death By Association

Merry Widow (A Lorne Simpkins short story)

It's A Dog's Life (A Lorne Simpkins short story)

A Time To Heal (A Sweet Romance)

A Time For Change (A Sweet Romance)

High Spirits

The Temptation series (Romantic Suspense/New Adult Novellas)

Past Temptation

Lost Temptation

Clever Deception (co-written by Linda S Prather)

Tragic Deception (co-written by Linda S Prather)

Sinful Deception (co-written by Linda S Prather)

PROLOGUE

*T*he night was crisp but thankfully dry. It was to be expected with Christmas just around the corner. Joshua had been at the pub for a couple of hours, mainly to get away from his nagging wife. His phone rang. He was tempted to ignore it, knowing that it was bound to be her. But after a brief consideration, he muttered a few expletives and removed it from his pocket.

Damn, woman, give me some peace for one night, will you?

"Hello, sweetheart."

"Joshua Smith, don't tell me you're still throwing pints of beer down that scrawny neck of yours. Have you seen the time?"

He paused under a streetlight and looked at his watch. "Oh dear, yes, it is rather late. You told me there was no rush to get home this evening, so why are you calling me now, demanding to know where I am?"

"For your information, I'm not *demanding* anything. All I'm doing is pointing out the facts... as usual. Why do you insist on going back on your word?"

"I'm not. Your parting words to me before I left the house

were, and I distinctly remember this, for me to have a good time and not to hurry back because you had a lot of work you needed to catch up on in the office this evening."

"Okay, you've got me there. Fortunately, I've completed all my paperwork and the housework I needed to do. How long are you going to be?"

"I'm five minutes from the house, unless you want me to turn back to the pub? You could nip out and join me there."

"No, I'll give it a miss. Don't be long."

His wife ended the call.

"I won't." He tucked his phone back into his jacket pocket, pulled up his collar to ward off the chill that was seeping into his bones now that he'd stopped walking, and prepared to set off again.

A man wearing a hooded jacket approached him from the other end of the alley.

"Evening, nice one for a stroll," Joshua muttered as the man passed him by.

The stranger mumbled something in response and strolled past. Joshua shrugged and set off again. He hadn't got far. Footsteps sounded behind him, and then he experienced a sharp pain in his lower back which forced him to his knees. He cast a glance over his shoulder to see the hooded man.

"You fucking scum. I told you I'd make you pay for what you did... one day."

"You! But why? How has it come to this? Help me, I need to get to the hospital."

Joshua reached out a hand for assistance, but the hooded man kicked his arm away with force and he ended up face-first on the ground. The pain in his back intensified, crippling him. He was stumped after having consumed one too many pints this evening to be thinking clearly.

The stranger stood over him and laughed. "I said you

wouldn't get the upper hand over me. You should have listened to the warnings. I gave you plenty of chances to back off. Bloody-minded, that's your trouble, and now look where it has led you. You'll never see your wife or son again, not now, not by the time I've finished with you."

The knife entered Joshua's body multiple times. He should have cried out for help, but the wind had been knocked out of him, all his faculties hampered by his lack of coherence.

Why did I drink so much? Was he there, at the pub? Watching me, waiting to pounce when the opportunity presented itself? My God, is this how my life is going to end? Five minutes from home, down a filthy alley?

The blade pierced his skin for what seemed to be the fiftieth time. He wasn't a religious man, but he was tonight as he sought God's forgiveness and His assistance to end his agony swiftly. He was aware there was no way back for him now, even if someone was to stumble across his body within the next ten minutes or so.

"You need to be taught a lesson. You're a nobody, you should have left well alone, then you wouldn't be in this mess, would you? A few more jabs and I'll leave you to die."

His assailant continued, jab after jab, until Joshua lay there, the light fading rapidly, his breath becoming more and more shallow. His final thoughts remained with his wife and their son. It had been a pleasure raising him, he was a chip off the old block for definite.

Farewell to both of you. I shall miss you. See you on the other side.

3

CHAPTER 1

*I*t had been a hectic evening so far. Mark had come home later than usual, leaving Sara to fend for them in the kitchen, her least favourite chore.

"I said I would knock something up when I got home. You needn't have gone to all this trouble, but I appreciate your efforts. It smells delicious."

"Not up to your fabulous standards, but I've done my best. Get cleaned up and I'll dish up the stir-fry before everything goes too far and looks limp."

"You worry too much."

"It's your fault. You're such an exceptional cook that anything I'm likely to serve up is crap in comparison."

"Nonsense. Says who? You will never hear me slating your attempts in the kitchen. I'll just have a quick wash and get changed, be down before you know it. Have we got rice or noodles with it?"

"I thought noodles would be better. Saying that, I think I've overcooked them."

"Have faith in your abilities. You're in control, that's all you have to remember. If you think things are cooking too fast, lower the heat or better still, turn it off. You don't have to have the pots constantly boiling all the time."

"I know. I've learnt that the hard way. This is the second pot of noodles I've cooked today."

He kissed her on the nose and inspected the pot. "See, they're fine. I'll be two ticks. You can start dishing up if you want."

"I'm a coward, I think you should do it."

He tutted and tore out of the kitchen. Sara boiled a kettle, ready to rinse the noodles. Mark's phone rang on the counter, and she was in a complete quandary whether to answer it or not. She placed the pot and sieve on the draining board and reached for it, but the phone fell silent. Mark came back into the room.

"Sorry, I tried to answer it, but I was too late."

He smiled. "You had your hands full. Want me to take over now? I wouldn't want to step on your toes, not when you're doing so well."

"Get away with you. I'm exhausted. Please do, I need to get myself a drink. Want a beer?"

"Wonderful. Whoever it was, I'll ring them back later."

Sara prepared the drinks and handed Mark his, but he politely rejected it.

"Pop it on the table, I'm otherwise engaged at the moment."

She gave an embarrassed chuckle and quickly laid the table, something she'd neglected to do whilst freaking out at the stove.

Mark served up their meals and carried the plates to the table. He took a sip from his lager and said, "This is fabulous. I'm fed up with you putting yourself down in the kitchen, there's nothing wrong with what you've created and, I repeat, you should have more faith in your abilities."

Sara blushed. "You did all the hard work, making it look

presentable."

"You're an idiot." He took a mouthful and sighed. "As expected, it tastes fine, more than fine..." His eyes widened, and his tongue ran the length of his lips. He downed half a bottle of lager before he spoke again. "Umm... did you put chilli in this?"

"Yes, why? Is it too much?" Sara hadn't had the courage to taste hers yet. She picked out a piece of chicken and nibbled at the corner, then swiftly dropped her fork and gulped down half a glass of wine. "Oh heck. Umm... in my defence, the stopper came off the bottle as I was shaking it."

Mark laughed and stood. He left the table and returned with the sugar canister and some crème fraîche. He added a spoonful of each to his dinner, stirred it and tasted it again.

"You're taking your life into your hands doing that, aren't you?" she asked, disappointed with her effort.

"It's fine now. Here, try it." He stuck his fork in and fed her some chicken and bean sprouts from his plate.

Reluctantly, she opened her mouth and was shocked at the difference. "Now that's passable."

He pulled her plate towards him, stirred in a spoonful of sugar and crème fraîche and gave it back to her. "Where there's a will. Eat it, it's fine."

They were halfway through their meal, enjoying it now that Mark had rescued it from being thrown in the bin. It was then that he decided to check his phone to see who the missed call was from.

"Who was it?" Sara sampled another mouthful of stir-fry.

"It was Dad. I'll give him a call back later, after I've done the washing-up."

"No, you won't, I'll do that. It must be urgent if he's calling you during the week."

Mark fell silent but continued to tuck into his dinner. He eventually pushed his plate to one side, the majority of his stir-fry eaten, and rang his father back. He put the phone on speaker. "Hey, Dad, how are you? Sorry for the delay, we were eating dinner."

"Ah, I wasn't sure if you'd be eating yet or not. We have some news for you. Maybe we should ring you back later, once you've completed your meal."

"No, it's fine. Sara's here, we're both listening. You sound concerned, what's wrong?"

His father sighed a few times.

Mark instinctively reached for Sara's hand. "Dad, you're worrying me now. Tell us what's going on."

"Okay, well, there's no easy way of telling you this... your mother hasn't been too well lately, having headaches and dizzy spells. I made her go to the doctor's last week. He sent her for an emergency CT scan when she stumbled and fell at the surgery."

"You never said. Oh God, what's wrong with her?"

"I'm all right, Mark, there's no need for you to worry, it's all in hand. I told your father not to ring you. You have your own life to lead. You don't want to hear all our woes when you have a hectic schedule yourself."

"Mum, that's enough," Mark quickly admonished her. "If there's something wrong, I need to know. What's going on?"

His grip tightened around Sara's hand. She smiled at him, but his expression remained one of concern for his mother.

"Mum?" he asked again.

"There's an abnormality in my brain, dear. I've got to go for further tests before they're willing to offer any kind of prognosis."

Mark closed his eyes and shook his head. Sara could tell the news wasn't good. Despite him being a vet, she knew he was aware of what was being said. Sara's heart lurched, and she could do little to prevent the tears from forming in her tired eyes.

"I'm sorry," she whispered.

He shook his head again and squeezed his lips tightly shut, as if afraid to speak.

"Mark, are you there?" his father asked.

"I'm here, Dad. I'm coming up to see you."

"No, I don't want that, Mark. You've got a practice to run. You told us only last week how snowed under you are, now there's a lack of vets in the area. I don't want to put you out, not at this stage, not when we're unsure what's going on," his mother insisted, her voice touched with emotion.

"I'll make a few calls. I want to be there, to offer you both my support. You shouldn't be going through this alone."

"I'm not alone, I have your father with me. Please, don't come yet. I have an appointment at the hospital on Friday with a neurosurgeon, we'll know more then."

"I'll get something sorted by then. I want to hear what the doctor has to say in person, Mum, not secondhand and watered down."

"I insist you should stay there. I'm aware you have a business to run and patients to care for. Your father will accompany me to the hospital. The last thing I wanted to do was worry you, Mark, but your father insisted that you should know, so, for a peaceful life, I agreed to ring you, but you have your own life to lead with the beautiful Sara."

"I'm not going to argue with you about this, Mum, I'm coming and that's all there is to it. I'll get things organised in the meantime. I'll be with you Thursday evening. I'll take Friday off, rearrange my appointments and be with you at around nine."

"I feel bad about disrupting your schedule like this," his mother replied on a sob.

"Liz, listen to me, you're not disrupting Mark's schedule. He wants to be there with you," Sara chipped in.

9

"The last thing I want to be is a nuisance to anyone," Liz replied. The sound of her crying came quickly.

Mark sat there, stunned, listening to his mother breaking her heart. Sara moved her chair closer to him, flung an arm around his shoulder and hugged him. At first, he stiffened, resisting the temptation for a cuddle. Sara knew how determined Mark could be, but eventually, he melted into her, and they hugged each other. When she pulled away from him, Sara could see the hurt swimming in his eyes.

"We're going to hang up now," his mother stated. "I don't want you dwelling on this, Mark. I'm not denying it won't be nice to see you, it's been a while since you ventured north, but only come if you can make adequate arrangements to cover the practice. You hear me?"

"Yes, Mum. What about the restaurant? Is someone running it for you?"

"Don't worry about that, it's all in hand. Speak to you soon. I want to assure you both that I feel fine in myself, it's the constant headaches that are getting me down."

"Keep taking the painkillers, Mum, they'll help," Mark advised.

"I'll do that. We love you both."

His mother ended the call before either Mark or Sara could respond. Mark hugged her tightly, and for the first time since she'd known him, he sobbed uncontrollably into her shoulder.

She rubbed his back and whispered, "Let it out, love. She'll be fine, I feel sure she'll get through this. We all will."

Eventually, he pulled away and wiped the tears from his cheeks. "Will we? I know the signs, what's involved, even though I'm a vet, I know what all of this means."

"You've got to push that aside for now, Mark, find the strength to help your mother through this."

He nodded and rested his head on her shoulder again.

There, they sat in silence for the next few minutes until he turned away from her and collected the plates.

"I'll do that. You have a lot to sort out with the practice. Why don't you make a start on that?"

"If you're sure. Thanks, Sara. I don't know what I'd do without you."

"It works both ways. Sorry the dinner wasn't up to scratch."

"It was fine, stop with the recriminations. You made the effort... sorry, that came out wrong. It was beautiful, a little more heat than we're used to, but that was resolved quickly enough, wasn't it?"

"Yes, my hero, you saved the day again."

"Hero, my arse. If that were the case, I'd be doing everything I could to save Mum, wouldn't I?"

"Let's not go there. You're going to do your best for her. She hasn't even had the diagnosis yet, so let's not jump ahead of ourselves."

He raised an eyebrow but refrained from speaking. Sara watched him walk out of the room, taking his phone with him, and she busied herself with cleaning up the mess she had created throwing their disastrous meal together. This was the part in the cooking process that she detested the most, what came after the creative method, not that there had been much to that side of things this evening, apart from her trying to kill them with red-hot chilli sauce that had no right featuring in a stir-fry. Naively, she had thought it would be a suitable substitute for oyster sauce that they had run out of. How wrong could she have been? Her throat still felt like she'd been practicing putting out fires with her tongue during a circus act that had gone terribly wrong.

She finished off in the kitchen and joined Mark in the lounge. He was on the phone. She squeezed onto the couch beside him and placed Misty, their cat, on her lap. Misty sensed there was something wrong; she wasn't her usual purring self either. Sara kissed the top of Misty's head and stroked her ears. Mark finished his call and rested his head back against the couch.

"As suspected, I can't find anyone to cover. I'm going to have to cancel the appointments for Friday and see what the weekend brings."

"Do you want me to take a few days off work to come with you?"

"No, you stay here. I'll be straight up and back, hopefully." He placed his hands over his face and let out a guttural groan. "Why now? And why Mum? That sounded awful, I didn't mean it to come out as though I wish this was happening to Dad…"

"I know you didn't mean it like that. Give yourself time to process what's happening. I'm sure your mother will be fine."

He looked at her and shook his head. "My gut is telling me otherwise."

"Then you're going to have to ignore it until you've seen the neurosurgeon with your parents."

The conversation died between them. Sara sensed Mark was in a reflective mood and left him alone. He exited the room ten minutes later. She went looking for him after a few minutes and found him in the bedroom, packing an overnight bag.

Sara sat on the end of the bed and asked, "Are you all right? Or is that a silly question?"

"I'm sorry, I don't think I can answer that right now, not honestly. I suppose I'm…"

"Go on, don't stop there. Tell me what's going on in that cute mind of yours."

He laughed. "Cute mind? If you say so. It's hard to put it into words really."

"Try, for me." She reached for his hand that was resting

on the bag.

He removed his hand and flopped onto the bed beside her. "I feel guilty."

"What? Wait! What the heck do you have to feel sorry for? I'm confused."

Mark placed his elbows on his knees and rested his head in his hands. "For not being there for my parents. How many times have we visited them since we've been together?"

Sara sighed and hooked an arm around his shoulders. "That's been a tough ask over the years, given our punishing schedules. Plus, your parents work just as hard as we do. How do you think this is going to affect the restaurant?"

He shrugged. "I don't know. Maybe Mum will need to consider selling up now. She's put her heart and soul into that place over the years, it's bound to have taken a toll on her health."

"You don't know that. It's true, she's been devoted to the restaurant, but I thought she told us last year that she'd employed a head chef, or did I imagine her telling us that?"

He paused and frowned. "Maybe, I can't remember. I feel bad about that, I should have been more attentive. Perhaps it was Mum's way of reaching out to me, and what did I do? I ignored her plea for help, if it was one, and now look where we are."

"You're thinking too deeply about this, love. Stop punishing yourself. Your mother wouldn't want to hear you speaking like this, would she?"

"But it's here." He clutched a hand over his heart.

"You're wrong. Don't do this to yourself. Take a step back and let's see what Friday brings."

"You don't get it, do you? I can't wait until Friday. I need to get my head in the right place before I travel to my parents' house. To sort out the options that will be open to Mum when the neurosurgeon confirms her worst fears."

"This isn't like you in the slightest, Mark. You're usually the most positive person I know. Far more positive than me most days."

"And look where it has got me."

She held out her arms to hug him again, but he pulled away from her and flew into the bathroom. Seconds later, the shower started running. Sara decided to leave Mark to it, give him the space needed to deal with this unprecedented predicament. She found herself wading like a duck far out in the ocean, unsure what to say or do for the best.

Coffee in hand, she returned to the lounge and flicked through the channels on the TV, pausing on the Sky News bulletin that was just ending. The weather map came up on the screen; another cold, often damp, few days ahead of them to look forward to. She thought how amazing it was that the weather almost always reflected the mood they were in, or did it? Was she guilty of overthinking again? She finished her coffee and snuggled up with Misty.

The movement of Mark sitting on the sofa beside her woke her a few minutes later.

"Sorry," he mumbled.

She inched closer to him and hesitantly rested her head on his chest. This time he didn't pull away from her. Instead, he kissed the top of her head and whispered an apology for his behaviour.

"You've got nothing to apologise for. Do you want to watch a film?"

"Not really. I'm willing to go with the flow if you want to see one."

Sara picked up the remote and dotted around the channels in search of a light-hearted comedy. They started and stopped a couple before settling on one they both agreed was passable. Within half an hour, they had both dozed off. Sara's phone rang, startling her.

She answered it, forcing herself awake enough to under-stand the caller.

"Sorry to interrupt your evening, ma'am, it's the control centre here. We've got an incident, and the pathologist asked me to give you a call. She's requesting your attendance at the scene."

"It must be bad if Lorraine has asked for me specifically."

"Yes, ma'am. Do you want the details?"

"Please, I'll get a pen and some paper, just a moment."

"Can't you have a bloody evening off for a change?" Mark snapped and marched out of the room.

His angry tone stunned her. She chose to ignore it and concentrated on getting the information down about the new case. "I'm ready."

"It's out in Belmont, ma'am. There's an alley at the bottom of Turnpike Road. Lorraine said that she will meet you there."

"Right, thank you. Can you contact DC Barry Thomas for me? He's my temporary partner at the moment."

"I'll do it now. Thank you and again, I apologise for spoiling your evening."

"You didn't, that had already been spoilt earlier. ETA twenty-five minutes."

"I'll pass the message on. Thank you, DI Ramsey."

Sara ended the call, sucked in a deep breath, ran her hand over Misty's head, and then went in search of Mark. She found him standing by the back door, gazing up at the night sky. "I doubt if you'll be able to see much out there tonight."

"How did you guess? Don't tell me you have to go out?"

"Yes, there's an urgent crime scene I need to attend."

"Why? Why does it always fall on your shoulders at night, after you've put in a full day's shift?"

"The pathologist requested my attendance, so she must feel it's a bad one. Don't make this harder than it needs to be.

She trusts me to do the right thing for the victims, I can't let her down."

"What about letting me down? I need you here with me tonight, Sara, more than I've ever needed you before... and here you are, running out on me."

Sara closed her eyes. The last thing she wanted or needed right now was to fall out with Mark, knowing that he would be leaving her in a couple of days to be with his mother. "Don't look at it that way, Mark, this could turn out to be a very important case. It's my job to get the criminals off the streets as swiftly as possible. Granted, it doesn't always work out that way, but my team and I can't do that if we're stuck at home, can we?"

"Just go. It's obvious your work means more to you than I do."

"That's unfair." She placed a hand on his forearm, and he tugged it away.

"Just go," he repeated.

Sara knew when to retreat. This was totally out of character for her husband, treating her this way, and she felt bad about leaving him, but she knew it was for the best. "Hopefully I'll be back before you know it."

"I doubt it. I'll be going to bed soon," was his parting comment.

He stormed out of the kitchen and thumped up the stairs. Leaving Sara feeling dispirited. She locked the back door, made sure Misty's bowls were topped up with food and water and that the cat litter tray was clean, then left the house. She didn't bother shouting goodbye to Mark, what was the point? She peered over her shoulder at the house and saw him watching her from the bedroom window. She waved, but he didn't respond.

. . .

BARRY HAD BEATEN her to the scene. He was standing by his car, suited and booted. "Evening, ma'am. Nice night for it?"

"Is it? I won't keep you long." She pulled on her suit and removed a pair of plastic shoe covers which she carried up the alley, once she'd signed the log at the cordon. "Thanks for coming out, Barry. I must admit, the woman on control caught me napping when she rang."

"I was seeing to Lilly, our daughter, at the time. She's been a little grizzly for a few days now. I told Gemma to get an early night."

"Ouch, sorry to hear that. I hope Lilly is better soon."

"Thanks. The trouble with kids is they can't tell you what's wrong, not really. Gemma thinks it's just a cold. I took Lilly's temperature earlier, and it was a fraction down, not much."

"Always best to keep a close eye on these things. Right, let's see what Lorraine has for us."

Lorraine was busy instructing her team. She saw Sara and Barry approaching and dismissed the techs. "Ah, there you are, better late than never, I suppose."

"It was our evening off. You're lucky we're here, so you can stop with the snide remarks. What have we got?"

"Get you. You know I'm only messing with you. Stop being so defensive."

Sara rolled her eyes. "It's been a bad evening, for both of us."

"Okay, well, I'd say your evening is about to get a lot worse."

"Meaning?"

"Come with me. My guys are about to erect the marquee to keep the weather at bay."

Sara's gaze drifted to the right, to where the victim's body lay on the ground. "How was he killed?"

"You'll see for yourself soon enough. You're going to need

to prepare yourselves for the worst."

Sara glanced sideways at Barry who was straining his neck to view the victim.

She dug him in the ribs. "Did you hear that? Prepare for the worst. I know you haven't attended many crime scenes over the years, so heed that warning, okay?"

"Yes, boss. So, it's a gruesome one then, is that what you're telling us, Lorraine?"

The pathologist stared at Barry for several seconds and then jerked a thumb in his direction. "Is he for real?"

Sara cringed. "Cut him some slack, he's used to cracking cases from his desk. This part of an investigation is all new to him."

"Whatever, you know my rules, DI Ramsey, no puking over the victim. I'm making sure you don't allow that to happen tonight."

"It won't. Will it, Barry?"

"I'm going to be the utter professional, boss, like always."

Sara glared at him, praying that his blasé attitude wasn't about to bite him in the arse once he'd laid eyes on the corpse. Knowing that Lorraine didn't issue these kinds of warnings willy-nilly was putting her on edge, more for her partner's sake than her own. Carla, her regular cohort, often suffered from having a dodgy tummy at a crime scene, depending on the severity of the victim's wounds.

"Ready for this?" Lorraine asked.

Sara and Barry both nodded and followed her down the alley.

"Wait," Sara said. "Who called it in?"

"The wife. She was the one who found him. She was standing next to her husband with her son when we arrived. I sent them home, told you'd call round to see them later. They're going to stay up and wait for you."

"Geez, I bet that was tough on her, or should I say them?

We'd better get round there ASAP." Sara turned to make her way back to the car, but Lorraine latched on to her arm.

"Not so fast, DI Ramsey. You need to see this with your own eyes to understand what the victim went through before he met his Maker."

"Jesus, I wasn't trying to get out of it, I had the family's best interests at heart. They must be going through hell right now."

"All you're doing at present is wasting my time."

Sara shrugged. "Unintentionally. Let's get this over and done with."

Barry watched on as her conversation with Lorraine became heated. Lorraine turned her back, expecting them to follow once more.

Sara could feel her stir-fry at the back of her throat. She was determined not to let it resurface, if only to save face in front of Barry. Lorraine's body blocked their view until she took a step to the right.

Sara's gaze immediately dropped to the victim. "Holy shit!" The acid burned her tonsils.

Lorraine tutted and said, "Didn't I tell you it was bad? Have I ever knowingly lied to you before?"

"Oh my, you're right about one thing, I've never seen anything like this before."

They heard a retching noise, and Sara instinctively pushed Barry away.

"I'm sorry, I can't…" he spluttered.

Lorraine gave Sara one of her looks. She threw her arms up in the air and let them slap against her thighs, her suit rustling in objection. "When will people start taking me seriously? I don't ask for much from you guys, do I? I did what I could to prevent this from happening, and yet, here we are, dealing with the fucking consequences."

Sara took a step towards Lorraine and jabbed her with

her elbow. Through gritted teeth, she said, "Give him a break. He's an excellent copper but he's not used to dealing with the victim side of things. You said yourself this is one of the most gruesome crimes you've had to deal with, so I'm asking you to cut him, and me, some slack."

"All right. You'd better deal with your partner before we proceed. The tech team are about to erect the tent anyway, so stand back."

"Thanks for being so sympathetic, Lorraine." Sara couldn't resist having one last dig at her friend.

She dashed across the alley to check how Barry was feeling. One of the techs had given him a wad of tissues. He was in the process of wiping his mouth.

"Are you all right?"

"Sorry to have let you down, ma'am. I've never seen anything quite like that before. I thought Lorraine was just saying it to wind us up, I didn't realise she meant it."

"It doesn't matter. How are you? Would you rather sit this one out and wait in the car?"

"No, I think I'll be all right now. It was the shock of… well, I don't have to go into details. May I ask why you weren't affected by it?"

"Hey, who said I wasn't? It's true, that was one of the worst things I've witnessed, but I suppose my stomach has hardened to it over the years. This is your first one, or one of your first, and it isn't pleasant, not by a long shot. The choice is yours: give it another go or sit this one out. Either way, I don't mind. On the other hand, Lorraine will curse you if you puke over the victim once the tent is up. Do you think that's a possibility?"

"I don't think I have anything left now, boss. I'd like to give it another try, if you'll allow me to."

"Any sign of you vomiting again, I need you to hot-foot it out of there, you hear me?"

"You have my word. One question: what kind of person would do that to another human being?"

"A sick individual. I fear we're going to have our work cut out for us with this investigation. We're all going to need to be on top form. Are you with me, Barry?" She thought about extending her hand to shake but quickly reconsidered.

"I'm with you all the way, boss. I'm embarrassed that I threw up, especially after Lorraine's warning. Does this mean that I'll be in her bad books now?"

"She forgives easily, don't worry. I've got your back if she comes down heavily on you."

"Thanks, boss, you're the best."

"I know. Come on, the tent is fully erected now, and if I know Lorraine, she'll be in there, arms folded, tapping her foot while she waits for us."

Barry took the hint, shoved the unused tissues in his pocket and gave her the thumbs-up. "I'm ready. It's the willing and able part that I'm not sure about."

Sara rubbed his arm. "Give it a shot. Keep your eye on the opening in case you need to make a swift exit."

"That's a deal. Sorry I let you down."

"You didn't. Chin up. Let's start afresh, imagine we've just arrived at the scene."

"Good advice."

Sara held the flap of the tent open, and they both entered. As she had predicted, Lorraine was in her usual pissed-off stance.

"It's about time. Are you feeling better now, Constable?"

"Yes, sorry about before, Lorraine."

"Ensure it doesn't happen a second time. Right, what we have here is a crime that denotes we're dealing with a brutal and vindictive killer. My first impression would be that the victim was known to them."

Lorraine knelt beside the body, and Sara followed suit

21

while Barry remained standing, close to the exit.

Sara noticed a few markers dotted around the area. "Dare I ask what they are for? Have you found any evidence of note at the scene yet?"

"I was wondering when you were going to ask about those. That's where his missing body parts were located."

"His what?" Sara scanned the victim's body briefly, noting all his limbs were intact, and then glanced at Lorraine.

She pointed to the victim's face, the blood that was masking where his ears had been removed. "One pair of ears and his tongue."

"What the fuck? His mouth has been crudely sewn up, so you're presuming that his tongue has been removed?"

"Exactly, unless we're looking for a second victim and the tongue belongs to them. As you can see, his eyes are closed, lots of blood around the cheek area. We haven't discovered them yet."

Lorraine spread open one of the eyelids, and Sara was confronted by a gaping hole.

"Oh shit!" Barry said and darted out of the tent.

Lorraine groaned. "You need to have a word; he's pissing me off."

"Give me a break. It's been a pig of a day. While I agree he's not Carla, he's a great second choice, you just need to give him a chance. Now, can we get this over with? I sense an even longer night ahead of both of us."

"Pardon me for breathing. Okay, back to it. While I was waiting for you, a couple of patrol vehicles turned up. One of them was a K9 officer. I took the liberty of asking him to search the rest of the alley, to see if his dog can find anything that may have been discarded by the killer."

"Excellent shout. Saves me placing the call. Going back to what you said earlier, you truly believe the killer knew the victim? And this wasn't a random attack?"

"The clues are there. There's also something else jumping out at me."

Sara studied the corpse again and shook her head. "Nothing obvious is hitting me in the face. Care to enlighten me?"

"All right, let's see if you get it from this… what orifices have been attacked?"

Sara screwed her nose up and asked, "What?"

Lorraine puffed out her cheeks. "Come on, get that brain of yours working."

"As I've already pointed out, you've caught me at the end of a very long day. Some might even call it a mind-numbing day. Do you want to give me another hint?"

Lorraine crossed her arms and tapped her foot. "Look at him. I mean really study him. Yes, he has lots of stab wounds, yet another indication the attack was overkill and that the killer knew him, but what else do you see?"

Sara chewed on her lip and gulped, sensing Lorraine was about to jump up and down on her foot if she didn't come up with a reasonable answer soon. "Er… I give in. Be gentle with me, I've got personal stuff I've been hit with this evening as well."

"Oh, do tell."

"Later. You first."

Lorraine pointed first to her eyes, then her ears, and finally to her mouth.

"Jesus, it's like drawing blood from a sodding stone. What the fuck are you going on about, woman?"

"Call yourself a professional detective, huh!"

Sara could feel her temper rising. "Less of the effing insults, I can do without them at this time of night."

"Okay, I've wound you up enough, but I haven't, not really."

Sara gestured for her pathologist friend to get on with it.

23

"See no evil, hear no evil..."

"Speak no evil. Holy crap, yes, I can see it now, no pun intended."

Lorraine slow clapped her. They both turned, hearing the flap being pulled back. Barry stood there, looking sheepish.

"Umm... permission to enter. I swear I'm all puked out now."

"Come in. Are you okay?" Sara asked. It was her turn to shoot Lorraine a warning glare. Her eyes widened, as if to emphasise her point.

"I must apologise once again," Barry said.

Sara patted him on the shoulder. "Why don't you wait in the car? I think we're nearly done here."

"Are we?" Lorraine said. "I thought we were just starting to get somewhere. Come in, I'm sorry if I put you under more pressure than was necessary."

"You didn't, the onus was on me. I'm fine now. I've given myself a good talking-to and the proverbial kick up the backside. I apologise for letting the side down, boss."

"Stop it. You haven't done that in the slightest. Why don't I bring you up to date on things in the car? We'll leave Lorraine to deal with the corpse while we visit the family before they start cursing us for keeping them up until the early hours of the morning."

Lorraine tilted her head and asked, "Do I have a say in this?"

"Are you telling me you're incapable of doing your job without us hanging around your neck?"

"Get out of here before either of us says something we're likely to regret."

Sara smiled, aware that she had won the argument, for once. "I'll look forward to reading your report."

"When I get the time to dictate it, should be in the next day or two."

Sara saluted her and shooed Barry backwards.

"Are you sure about leaving the scene this early?" he whispered.

"Most definitely. I've had my share of Lorraine this evening to last me the whole month." She marched on ahead of him and stripped off her protectives which she deposited in the black bag at the cordon.

"Did I miss something?"

"Leave it, for now. Hop in, we've got a heartbreaking interview ahead of us."

"You're intent on putting me through the wringer this evening, aren't you?"

"Not intentionally, it just worked out that way. How's your stomach now?"

"All better. Thanks for being patient with me, boss, not every DI would have backed me the way you have this evening. I appreciate it."

"Nonsense. We all have bad days at the office now and again, it's how we overcome them that matters, never forget that, Barry. Learn from your mistakes and you'll be fine."

"You mean grow a stronger stomach, don't you?"

Sara laughed. "That as well."

SARA PULLED up outside the detached house at the end of an estate which, according to Barry, had been built around fifteen years earlier. The garden was low maintenance, slate beds on either side of the path with large containers dotted here and there. The downstairs was all lit up, curtains drawn in the front room.

"Are you ready for this?" she asked.

Barry smiled and nodded. "I won't let you down again. I have my professional head screwed firmly in place now."

"Glad to hear it, not that I think you've let me down

tonight. Let's forget about it and move on."

"I'm up for that."

He rang the bell, and they both inhaled and exhaled a few deep breaths to steady their nerves.

A young man in his mid-to-late twenties opened the door, his blond hair spiky in places as if he'd spent the last few hours running his sweaty hands through it. "Yes, who are you? Oh wait, are you the police?" His eyes narrowed.

Sara and Barry produced their warrant cards.

"We are. DI Sara Ramsey and DC Barry Thomas. Would it be possible to come in and speak with you?"

A woman's voice called out from behind the man, "Who is it, Allan? What do they want?"

"It's all right, Mum. The police have finally shown up."

"Oh. Don't leave them standing on the doorstep, not on a night like this."

He took a step back and made a sweeping gesture with his right arm. "Come in."

"Thanks," Sara said. She hesitated about removing her shoes. Instead, she dried them thoroughly on the doormat.

Barry did the same, and he closed the door behind him.

Allan showed them into the lounge where his distraught mother was rocking back and forth in a high-backed armchair, next to the gas fire.

"I can't remember your names, sorry," Allan apologised.

Sara smiled weakly at the woman then introduced herself and Barry.

"I don't care about your names, all I'm bothered about is getting the bast... excuse my language, the person who did this to my husband. My wonderful, caring husband, who did everything he could to make our family feel comfortable."

"Would it be okay if we sit down?" Sara asked.

"Yes, sorry. Please take a seat. I found him. In that damn alley. I rang him when he was walking home. Did I distract him? Allow the person to jump on him? He told me he wouldn't be long. I left it half an hour and then went looking for him. I'll never forget this night, never. Finding him like that."

"I'm so sorry for your loss. It must have been a dreadful shock for both of you when you discovered him. Are you up to answering a few questions for us?"

"I have dozens of questions of my own to ask. Will you be able to answer them?" the woman asked.

"Sorry, I don't know your name."

"It's Gail. This is Allan, our only son, and my husband is, or should I say was, Joshua Smith." She shook her head over and over. "I'll never be able to unsee what I saw tonight, never in a million years." Her hand tightened into a ball, and she rested it against her lips, doing her best to hold herself together.

Allan sat on the edge of the chair and flung an arm around her shoulders.

"Are you all right, Mum? Try not to let it consume you. You need to let it go in order to get on with your life. Remember him as he was... not how we saw him in the alley."

Tears cascaded down his mother's cheeks, and she glanced up at him. "I know you're talking sense, darling, but this is so difficult for me to get my head around. The thought of him never coming through that front door again, that's what is crippling me. I know in my heart that I will never see him again, have a conversation with him over the dinner table, like we used to. Go on holidays together. I feel so numb. My insides are twisted into a giant knot, I'm not sure I know how to get rid of it. I've never felt so alone as I do at this moment. We've been together for over thirty years, for him to be taken from me in such a despicable way... how will we cope without him, Allan? How?"

Sara was happy to leave the mother and son to have their conversation without interrupting, gleaning what she could from what they both had to say.

"Mum, we're going to need to be extra-strong, stronger than we've ever had to be in our lives before. It's what Dad would have wanted, isn't it?"

"He would have. It doesn't mean that it's going to hurt any less, son. God, the sight of him lying there, bleeding to death. No one deserves to go out that way, no one."

Allan pulled his mother tighter against his chest and let her cry. "It's all right, Mum, let it all out."

"You say your husband spoke to you on the phone for a while before his death," Sara said. "Can you tell me if he sounded distressed at all?"

"No, he was walking home from the pub. Maybe he was a little bit tipsy, not enough to alter his speech, but maybe it hampered his decision-making. Why did he come home that way? Walk down that alley when it was pitch-black? I know there are streetlights down there, but even so, there are patches that aren't lit well, anyone could jump out on you."

"How did he sound on the phone?"

"Okay. He'd had a good time at the pub and was keen to get home from what I could tell. Do you think someone attacked him on purpose? Were they aware of the route he took and pounced on him, or is that me overthinking things?"

"Possibly. The pathologist's initial findings are that he might have known his attacker."

Allan's head quickly turned in Sara's direction. "What? How can the pathologist know that?"

"Because of the ferociousness of the attack. She believes that your father knew the killer as it was frenzied, and he suffered lots of wounds. Attacks such as this mean raw emotions are involved, hence the knowing each other aspect."

"You're not just talking about the knife wounds, are you? It's the other ones that you're referring to... you know, the injuries that were done to his face."

"Possibly. At the moment that's pure speculation, but at this stage, we're regarding it as a good lead to delve into. Perhaps you can tell us if your father has fallen out with anyone lately?"

"No, not that I can think of," Gail replied instead of her son.

"Can I ask if your husband still worked?"

"Oh, yes, he ran his own accountancy firm in the city."

Working on his own initiative, Barry took out his notebook and jotted down the relevant information.

"What's the name of the business?" Sara asked.

"Smith's Accountancy, it's just up the road from Marks and Spencer."

"I think I know it. How long has your husband owned the business?"

"He used to work elsewhere, at Lawler's, on the outskirts of the city. He decided to start up his own firm around ten years ago. He was very successful at it, too."

"How many staff did he employ?"

"Another accountant and two secretaries. It's a small business but getting busier every year."

"And the name of the other accountant?"

"Ralph Bates. He joined Joshua about two years ago. That's right, isn't it, Allan?"

"Yes, I think so, but then, time whizzes past, doesn't it?"

"We'll check it out. Has your husband had any concerns to do with the business lately? By that I mean, has he had any trouble with clients or from a rival firm perhaps?"

The mother and son looked at each other and shook their

heads.

"Not that I can recall," Gail said after a moment's hesitation.

Allan left his seat and, agitated, he paced the floor. "Are all these questions necessary?"

"I'm afraid so. It's important for us to search for any possible leads from the outset. I'm sure you can understand that. At present, we've got little to nothing to go on."

He retook his seat and hugged his mother again. "I'm sorry," he mumbled, his eyes averting Sara's.

"There's really no need. I recognise how frustrating all of this must be for you, especially so soon after your father's death. What about neighbours? Have you fallen out with any of them lately?"

"No, we've always got on well with them, since the day we moved in, about two years ago."

"That's great to hear. It seems a nice area. All the properties appear to be well maintained, unlike some of the other older estates around here. What about family members? Do you have anyone else living close by?"

"No, there was just the three of us. We've had to say farewell to our respective parents over the past five years, through one illness or another, cancer, dementia, you name it, and it has touched our family with a vengeance. But we'd all survived, until this..." Gail said, her voice catching on a sob.

"Let it out, Mum, it's the only way you're going to heal."

Gail clutched her son's hand and lifted it to her lips. "I'm glad I've got you by my side, Allan. I wouldn't be able to cope if you weren't here."

Sara again watched the interaction between the mother and son for a few seconds then asked, "What about you, Allan? Any problems that you've had to deal with lately that might have transferred to your father?"

"Transferred to my father? What the hell is that supposed to mean?" Again, he jumped to his feet and paced the floor beside his mother.

She reached out a hand to him. He latched on to it, and she pulled him down to sit alongside her again.

"Just answer their questions. We want this over and done with quickly. We both need to get some rest. We'll have a busy day ahead of us tomorrow, sorting out your father's funeral."

Sara raised a hand. "I would hold off doing that just yet. The pathologist will need to perform a post-mortem on your husband first."

"Oh my, are you telling me that he'll need to be cut open?"

"It's a matter of procedure, once a crime of this nature has been committed."

"Christ, could this night get any worse?" Allan said. "Hasn't that man been through enough? Now you're telling us that the pathologist is going to depths that the killer never reached. Opening up my father. I can't believe this is true. Why? Haven't we suffered enough already? Why put my mother through all this pain and misery? What in God's name is it going to prove?"

"I'm sorry. Like I said, it's procedure. A victim's body can give the investigation team further clues that we can chase up and, nine times out of ten, performing a post-mortem will lead us to the killer and the motive behind the reason they took the victim's life… in this case, your father's life. I appreciate how upsetting this must be for you both, but it's an integral part of any investigation."

"Why don't you just get on with it then? Why tell us about it?"

Sara shrugged. "You have a right to know what's about to happen in the immediate future."

"Please, Allan, don't kick off. I should have realised this

31

would be the case. I think I've had enough now. My mind is shot, and my body is tired. I was exhausted before I set off and went looking for your father, that was hours ago."

Sara nodded. "We've asked all the questions we need to ask for the time being. I'll leave you my card. If you think of anything else that we failed to cover during the interview, please don't hesitate to get in touch."

She rose from her seat, and Allan accompanied them to the door.

"Inspector, please find the person responsible for robbing us of my dear husband. He was a wonderful husband and father to our son, he didn't deserve to die, not the way he died tonight. Alone and in a filthy alley," Gail said.

"Don't worry, Gail, you have my assurance that my team and I will do our very best for you."

"Thank you. Will you keep us updated during the investigation?"

"Yes, as best as I can. Take care of yourself and each other."

"Thank you. Allan is a good son, he won't let me down."

Sara smiled and left the room.

Allan was standing in the hallway with the front door open. "You need to catch this bastard, and soon, Inspector. I've heard too many scare stories in the press lately about lacklustre policing. I'm warning you now, I won't think twice about making a complaint if you fail in your duties."

Sara rocked on her heels at the force of his words. "At least give us a chance to get the investigation going before you think badly of us, Allan."

"I'm sorry, you're right, I should give you a chance. Let's face it, the press is having a field day with your lot at the moment, and I don't think I'm alone doubting the Force's capabilities, am I?"

"For your information, I don't believe the police skills in

this area have been questioned of late. Speaking for myself and my team, our success rate has been exemplary over the years. Only last year I got a personal commendation from the commissioner. I assure you, he doesn't hand those out like Smarties, far from it."

"Forgive me, I wasn't aware of that. All I'm doing is looking out for my mother. She's been through enough the last couple of years, losing her parents and then Dad's parents as well. That kind of sorrow begins to take a toll on a person."

"It's admirable that you're standing here, protecting your mother, but at this stage in the proceedings, there's really no need for you to do that. What you need to do is give us a chance. The investigation began the second we attended the crime scene. I'm warning you now, these things take time. There won't be an instant fix to this problem. We're going to make a start on things first thing in the morning, only because of the time of day, it's not in our remit to wake people up at this time of night, plus, we've both been on duty since first thing this morning."

"I understand what you're saying, but looking at things from our perspective, you sitting back tonight is only allowing the killer to get away. What if he's got a taste for it and is out there, on the prowl for his next victim?"

"That's a risk every detective has to take. We have to follow procedures, to work the case as we see fit at the time. I know from experience, working on hundreds of cases over the years, that we get further with clear heads and during daylight hours. Of course, if we have to work in the evenings further down the line during the investigation, then we'll do that as well. What I refuse to do is bang on people's doors at this time of night, just to ask them a few basic questions. Please, trust us, leave the investigation to us while you take care of your mother." She stepped out of the front door and turned to face Allan once more. "You have my word, we won't let you down. I'm not in the habit of failing victims' families."

"Glad to hear it. I'd better get back to Mum. I don't think it's truly hit her yet, nor me, come to that. I apologise for coming across as bolshy. I'm sure you'll understand my emotions are all over the place this evening, having just lost my father. It's the manner of his death that is rocking my world tonight."

"I can only imagine what you're going through. You and your mother will have our support throughout. Reach out if you need us, you've got my card."

"Thank you." He closed the door.

Sara got to the end of the path and expelled a deep breath. "That was a close one."

"Boss?"

"I'm glad I managed to calm him down. I've witnessed and been on the end of things escalating quickly in the past, and I can tell you, it wasn't pleasant. Right, let's get you back to your car."

"What did you make of the son?"

"Shall we say that he appears to be the protective sort?"

"And some. I thought the way he spoke to you was bang out of order, you know, having only just met you."

"It happens, Barry, you'll need to get used to dealing with people's anger whilst out in the field, it's far from a rarity these days."

"I don't suppose I'll ever get used to it. When are people going to realise that we're not the enemy? That we put our lives on the line to track down these villains? Carla's accident a few months ago is a prime example of that, isn't it?"

"True. We need to assess every investigation and the people we meet during a case separately; there's no 'one cap fits all' in this scenario and there never will be."

34

"I get that. What I'm struggling to get my head around is the way people think they can speak to a police officer. Christ, when I was a kid, I used to crap myself when a cop car passed me in the street."

Sara smiled. "You're a good person, Barry, don't ever change."

"I need to add something to what I've just spouted."

"Go on."

"It wasn't through having a guilty conscience either. I used to be genuinely scared of the police, didn't you?"

Sara paused to consider his question. "I suppose so. I've never really sat back and thought about it before. Sign of the times perhaps. People's anger dictating how they deal with others."

"Yeah, my mum is always telling me to be careful out here as the world has become such an angry place to live in, since Covid struck. I think she's right."

"I think she is, too. Something has drastically changed in our society over the years, and not for the better either. Still, all we can do is our very best and try to extinguish any volatile situations as swiftly as possible."

Sara dropped Barry back at the scene to pick up his car and then headed home for the evening. She crept into the house and went into the kitchen. There, she poured herself a glass of wine and texted Lorraine to tell her she was back home. She also told her that she had dropped in to interview the family, but they couldn't come up with any reason why Joshua Smith should have been targeted, effectively putting Lorraine's theory in doubt.

Lorraine messaged back a few minutes later with four words: *Lucky you, speak tomorrow.*

Sara sighed and opened the back door. She stared up at the sky. Now that it was clear, there were plenty of stars to mesmerize her. She was so caught up in the glittering display that she hadn't heard the kitchen door open. The first she knew she wasn't alone was when a hot breath touched her neck. She jumped and lashed out, catching Mark on the arm with force.

"What the hell, Sara? Why are you so jumpy all the time?"

She placed a hand on his cheek. He flinched and took a step backwards.

"I'm sorry. It wasn't my fault, you snuck up on me. I thought you'd be in the land of nod by now."

"I heard you come in, and when you didn't come straight to bed, I presumed something must be wrong. Pardon me for being concerned about you. I didn't mean to scare you."

"I'm sorry for being oversensitive. You caught me in a world of my own."

He gathered her in his arms and snuggled his face against hers. "What's going on between us?"

Sara pulled away from him and frowned. "I wasn't aware that anything was wrong. Are you implying there is?"

He released his arms and threw them up in the air. "I don't know. I think things have been on the edge for us for a few months now, at least that's how it has seemed to me."

"This is news to me, Mark. I've been under pressure, more so than normal, with Carla being off sick. I wasn't aware that it had caused any problems as such between us." Unexpected tears misted her eyes, but it was the fact that Mark was refusing to look at her that hurt the most. "Do you want to discuss this?"

"No, I'm tired. Are you coming to bed?"

Before she could reply, he marched towards the door and mumbled, "Either come with me or don't, I'm past caring."

The door slammed.

What the hell is going on? What have I done? Is this more to do with what's happening with his mother? Or are there problems between us that I have missed?

CHAPTER 2

*M*ark was up and dressed early the next day, before Sara had a chance to even open her eyes. After the front door slammed, she glanced at the clock; it was only six forty-five. He hadn't mentioned that he was intending to set off for work at the crack of dawn and, as far as she knew, he hadn't received an emergency call, requesting his attendance at the surgery. So, what the hell was going on with him?

Rather than dwell on all the negative thoughts bouncing around in her head, Sara decided to jump into the shower and make her way into the station. Something about catching an early worm came to mind.

With Misty fed and her tray cleaned, Sara made a fuss over her furry companion and swiftly bolted down a piece of toast with marmalade and a cool cup of coffee with an added splash of milk. Halfway through it, she regretted not having a warm cup, c'est la vie. She arrived at the station a few minutes before eight. Judging by how panicked he seemed, Sara presumed the desk sergeant, Jeff, had only just come on duty himself.

"Morning, ma'am, you're up with the larks today."

"I know. A new case dropped into my lap late last night, and I wanted to get things organised for the team before their shift starts."

"Ah, good for you. Anything I can do? What type of case?"

"A bad one. The victim was torn to shreds. Actually, you can check if the K9 found anything last night, if you would?"

Jeff checked the system and then rifled through some paperwork sitting in his in-tray, off to the left. "Ah, I do have something here. Oh my, this can't be right, can it?" His head rose, and he stared at her.

"What's wrong?"

"It says here that PC Blake found a pair of eyes in a nearby bin. Is this true?"

"Yes, sadly the victim had both ears and eyes removed, and his tongue. The only parts missing from the scene were his eyes. The pathologist instructed PC Blake to search the area. Glad he found them. Nothing like delivering an incomplete body back to a family."

"Quite right. When you said you had a bad case on your hands, you weren't kidding. Fancy mutilating someone like that." He shuddered and tidied up his paperwork.

"Exactly. I sense this is going to be a tough case to crack but, crack it we will. I must get on."

"Good luck. Don't forget, I'm here if you need me."

"Always good to know, Jeff."

Sara punched in her code to gain entry through the security door and headed up the stairs, her thoughts flipping between what was going on with her marriage and what she needed to do to get the case underway. As usual, once she hit her office, the case became her priority. Ignoring the huge pile of post on her desk, some of which had been hanging around for the past few days, she withdrew her notebook and jotted down a couple of pointers that she needed to make to the team when they eventually arrived for duty. That done, she nipped out to make a coffee at the drinks station, finding a caffeine-induced state always helped when tackling some of the nonsensical post that came her way.

The folks at head office need to get a life, like the rest of us. Hmm... is that true? Do I have a life of my own? Surely, if I did, my marriage wouldn't be in the mire, would it?

"Hello, you. I'm back."

A familiar voice she hadn't heard around the office for a couple of months forced her out of her reverie.

Sara ran to the door. "Carla. My God, it's so good to see you. I must admit, it had slipped my mind you were due back today."

"Charming. Three months enforced rest and recuperation and you've already forgotten about me."

"Nonsense. Have I heck. Take a seat, join me for a coffee, and we'll have a quick catch-up before the others get here." Sara guided her partner to the chair.

Carla removed her arm from Sara's. "Stop treating me like I'm an invalid. The doctor gave me the all-clear to return to work early because I've made a 'miraculous recovery'— they're his words, not mine. I really don't want any special treatment, either from you or the rest of the team. I've worked hard over the last few months to regain my fitness."

Sara smiled, left the office, prepared Carla a coffee and returned. The break gave her the opportunity to choose her words carefully. "Physically you may be okay, but what about up here?" She retook her seat and tapped her temple.

"I'll have you know that I'm fine in that department as well. At least I think I am. We're not likely to find out until I'm out there, in amongst it all again."

"I trust you. Hey, a new case came our way last night. Barry and I got the call to attend a murder scene. I won't go into the finer details with you, I'll save that for the team meeting, but it's a gruesome one. If you want to take a step back on this one and let Barry continue as my partner, I'm okay with that."

"Is that your way of telling me you don't think I'm up to it?"

"I didn't say that at all, nor would I. I do, however, think it makes sense for you to ease yourself back in around here after what's happened."

"That's where we differ. I could think of nothing worse than sitting around here, doing mundane tasks, while you're out there doing all the nitty-gritty stuff."

Sara smiled and tilted her head. "God, it's good to have you back. I'll have a quiet word in Barry's ear when he gets here. I have a feeling he'll willingly accept the demotion, after what he went through last night."

Carla frowned. "Meaning what?"

"He pissed Lorraine off at the scene."

Carla winced and picked up her mug. "Oh no, he didn't do the dreaded 'vomiting at the scene' trick, did he?"

"You've got it in one. I know you've had a few dodgy moments over the years, but yes, he definitely topped your efforts."

They both laughed.

"Poor sod," Carla said. "How's he done in general, filling in as your partner?"

"He's come on in leaps and bounds. He was a little hesitant at first, but it didn't take him long to get into the role."

"Was my position ever in doubt?"

"Never. You and I are the A-Team, and we always will be."

Carla sipped her drink and then let out a sigh. "It's great to be back. It's funny, isn't it? You detest the place when you're here, but when you're forced to stay away, you miss it like hell."

"It gets into your soul. I feel the same way when I'm on holiday."

"And how's Mark?"

Sara chewed on her lip. "That's another topic I think we should steer clear of at the moment."

"Sounds ominous. Are you guys okay?"

"I think so. What I can tell you is that Mark has to go back home to see his parents at the weekend because they believe his mother has a brain tumour."

Carla sat forward. "What? Is it bad?"

"I think the words 'brain tumour' strike terror into most of us. She's got an appointment to see the neurosurgeon on Friday. He'll tell her the full extent of what's going on then."

"Heck, poor Mark. I bet his mind is all over the place with that terrifying news."

"I suppose. But I think there's something else wrong with him, I just can't put my finger on what it can be. It'll sort itself out, in time. What about Des? I've seen him around a few times in the past week or so but haven't had the chance to stop and have a conversation with him."

"He's been amazing. Attentive throughout. So glad you hooked me up with him."

"Ah, nice to hear you admit that at last. He's definitely one you need to hang on to. I think every couple should go through a major incident before they walk down the aisle, if only to see how the other person reacts when adversity comes knocking."

"A bit extreme, but yes, I'm inclined to agree with you on that score. He's been my rock. Made sacrifices that I wouldn't have expected him to have made just to ensure my recovery never wavered. I couldn't ask for a better partner."

Sara wiped away the tear that landed on her cheek. "Crap, this is not how I planned to start my day, in tears. Seriously, I couldn't be happier for you both. Sorry you had to postpone the wedding. Did you get your money back from the venue you'd booked?"

"Yes, they accepted the excuse we gave them and issued a full refund."

"Excuse? It was hardly that. Your life was in the balance for a time."

"A tad over the top. It doesn't matter, we got the money back, that's all that counts."

"Have you sorted out another date yet?"

"We've decided not to be so extravagant and to do the wedding on the cheap, less stress that way. We're having a registry wedding instead."

"Hey, it makes sense to me. Weddings cost a fortune these days, and for what? A few hours of enjoyment when that money could be put to good use elsewhere, like setting up your forever home."

"Yeah, I agree. Can't believe some people spend twenty to thirty grand on their big day, it's crazy!"

A knock on the door interrupted their conversation, and Barry poked his head into the room. "Hey, Carla, it's great to have you back." He seemed genuinely relieved to see her.

Sara picked up there was something wrong. "What's up, Barry? Everything all right at home?"

"Not really, boss. Umm... I know the timing is shit... I was wondering if I could take a couple of days off."

Carla rose from her seat. "Here, sit down, Barry. I'll leave you guys to it."

"You don't have to go, Carla. It's Gemma, she missed her step last night and ended up falling down the stairs."

"Oh no. Did it happen while you were attending the scene with me?" Sara asked, the guilt rising.

"Yes, Lilly was having a bad night, she woke Gemma up, wanting a glass of water. Gemma was still half asleep and took a tumble. Luckily, I was on my way home when she rang me. We spent the night at the hospital in A and E. She's got her leg in plaster now."

"Ouch, she broke her leg?" Carla asked.

"Yes. I need to look after Lilly for a few days, just until she gets used to being in a cast. Sorry if it's inconvenient, boss, I can't see any way around it."

"Don't be silly. Of course you should take time off. You shouldn't have come in, you should have rung me first thing instead."

"Not the way I like to do things, boss. I'd rather come in and let you know face to face."

"Off you go. Ring me later with an update, if you wouldn't mind, and send Gemma our love."

"I will. Thanks for being so understanding. Sorry I'm letting you down like this."

"You're not, so get that out of your head."

Barry smiled, nodded then shot out of the room.

"Well, that settles it."

Carla's brow furrowed. "What does?"

"You're going to have to take up the reins and become my partner again, whether you like it or not."

"Seems that way, doesn't it? Poor Barry, he seems really concerned about Gemma. I was sorry we couldn't make it to his wedding. Did it go okay?"

"Yes, they had the perfect day. Hey, you need to have a word with them, they did theirs on the cheap."

"Good idea. I'll do that when he comes back to work. I'd better leave you to get on with your dreaded paperwork. Do you want me to do anything out there?"

"You can prepare the whiteboard for me. I'll deal with some of these, the rest can wait. I've got the perfect excuse now for neglecting my duties as we're going to be a man down for the foreseeable future."

"That one definitely fell into your lap at an opportune

moment."

Sara grinned and watched her partner leave the room, slower than normal.

Shit, if it's not one thing it's another. So much for hitting the ground running with this case. Looks like it's going to be hampered from the word go. I need to ensure that doesn't happen. Not with a vile killer on the loose.

"IN A NUTSHELL, THAT'S IT, FOLKS," Sara said. She placed the marker on the narrow shelf at the bottom of the board. "What we need to do is carry out the normal background checks on the family. We spoke with the wife and son late last night; they couldn't shed any light on who the likely suspect might be. According to the pathologist, a frenzied attack such as this one would have been carried out by someone known to the victim. All we need to do is find out who that person is."

"Simple, right?" Carla said.

"Yeah, we'll see. How remiss of me, slapped wrist. What I should have done at the beginning of this meeting was to welcome Carla back into the fold. I know you guys will give her all the support she's going to need to get back into the swing of things. It's unfortunate that Barry has been forced to take time off through personal matters, so I'm going to need you all to put in an extra effort on this case. This contemptable individual needs to be caught as quickly as possible. Carla and I will head out to the victim's place of work, see what we can unearth there. Other than that, there's not a lot to be done."

"What about CCTV footage around the area, boss?" Craig asked.

Sara screwed up her nose. "I might be mistaken but I don't think there's going to be much going on around there,

Craig. I'd love you to prove me wrong with a caveat: don't spend too much time on that angle. I say that only because the crime took place in an alley, off the beaten track. With one man down, I think your talents can be put to better use elsewhere."

"I've got you, boss. I'll do what's necessary and have a fleeting look at the cameras later, how's that?"

"Sounds good to me, thanks, Craig. Right, are you ready to go, Carla?"

"I am. Let's get this show on the road."

"Hey, that's usually my line. I'll let you off this time."

AFTER PARKING in Tesco's car park, they walked down the lane to the accountancy firm.

"We could always have lunch at the nice little café around the corner." Carla winked.

"Cheeky sod, and who would pay for that?"

"Ah, yes, I never considered that part. I'm a bit short until payday comes around."

"I thought you might say that. I suppose I owe you one, after putting yourself in harm's way and suffering the consequences for the past three months. We'll see what the morning brings first."

"You don't owe me anything. I was hurt in the line of duty."

"We'll argue the toss later. Here it is, I thought it was around here somewhere." Sara pushed open the door to a single-fronted narrow building.

A woman in her late fifties glanced up from the paperwork she was dealing with and raised a finger. "I'll be with you shortly."

"No rush," Sara called back.

45

She and Carla took a seat in the reception area. No sooner had they sat down than the woman approached them.

"Sorry to keep you waiting. We're a person short today and snowed under with work. How can I help?"

Sara and Carla stood and showed their IDs for the woman to study.

"DI Sara Ramsey and my partner, DS Carla Jameson. Would it be possible to speak with Ralph Bates, please?" It felt good introducing Carla as her partner again.

"Oh, I see. I'm afraid he's in a meeting for the next ten minutes or so. Do you want to wait for him?"

"Yes, we'll do that."

"Very well. Can I get you a drink while you wait?"

"Thanks. Two coffees would be great, milk and one sugar in each."

"I'll be right back, and you're welcome."

Sara and Carla returned to their seats. Sara withdrew her notebook from her pocket and flipped it open to a clean page. She jotted down the questions she intended to ask Bates once he became available.

"Would it be worth having a chat with the staff first?" Carla suggested.

Sara shook her head. "I'd rather not. I wouldn't appreciate someone speaking to members of my workforce without getting the all-clear first. We just need to be patient. It seems a busy firm, judging by what the receptionist had to say."

A man in a dark pin-striped suit appeared and held the door open for an elderly woman using a walking frame. "Don't worry, Edna, we'll get that sorted for you right away. Thank you for bringing it to my attention. I'll have a word with Joshua as soon as he's free."

"Thank you, Mr Bates. You're very kind. You all are here, that's why I enjoy coming down here to see you once in a while, especially as I don't tend to get out much these days."

"It's always a pleasure to see you. Why don't you treat yourself to a cuppa and a piece of cake at the café over the road?"

"Yes, yes, I think I'll do that. It's not like I have anything to rush home for, is it?"

Bates smiled and shook the woman's hand then closed the door behind her. He glanced in Sara's direction and gave a brief nod.

The receptionist brought their drinks and flew after Bates. She returned a few moments later. "Mr Bates says he can spare you five minutes. I'll show you through to his office. You can bring your drinks with you."

Sara and Carla picked up their cups and saucers and followed the woman through the small corridor to a large office at the rear.

Mr Bates welcomed them with a wary smile. "You wanted to see me? Please, take a seat."

"Sorry to descend on you unannounced. We appreciate you seeing us at such short notice. We won't keep you too long."

"Always happy to assist the police, not that I've had many dealings with you in the past. How can I help?"

"Umm... I'm assuming that Joshua's family have been in touch with you this morning?"

"Yes, Gail rang me at home, first thing. To say I was shocked would be an understatement. I still don't think it has sunk in. I've only told the staff. As you can probably tell, I have no intention of telling the clients what has happened, because basically, we don't really know yet, do we?"

"Very wise. There's no point causing any more upset than is necessary."

"Shocking state of affairs. I can't believe Gail was the one who found him. By the sounds of it, she appears to be holding it together well, but then, she's got Allan by her side, he's a good lad."

"It's going to be a tough few days for both of them. The reason we're here is to ask if Joshua had fallen out with anyone lately. Perhaps a client of his?"

"Hardly, he was a decent man. I've enjoyed my time working with him over the years."

"It seems to be a thriving business. Are you a partner in the firm?"

"No, there was talk of me becoming a partner, but I've had trouble finding the funds. What with the kids going off to university, all my spare cash has gone towards their living expenses."

"I see. That can be expensive."

"You're telling me. Do you have any idea who would have killed him?"

"Not so far, it's still very early days. Can you tell us more about the business and the staff? I'm aware that we're against the clock here."

"Yes, sorry. The day is pretty much fully booked. It was Joshua's idea to get all the clients in for a review."

Sara frowned. "You say that as if it is against the norm. Is it?"

He sighed and glanced out of the window on his left. "You could say that. I suppose you're going to find out soon enough, so I'd rather not be accused of deceiving you. There's another reason I haven't put my hand in my pocket to buy into the business."

"Oh, care to enlighten us?" Sara said, her heart rate increasing at the news.

"The firm is in financial trouble, hence the reason Joshua has made these extra appointments for most of the clients."

"I see. What are we talking about here, the firm possibly going out of business?"

"Yes, there's a great risk of that happening."

Sara inclined her head. *Maybe there's more to this case than meets the eye after all.* "Is there a reason for that?"

"You tell me, because I'm getting the feeling that Joshua failed to keep me informed, only did it when it suited him."

"Do you have access to the business' accounts?"

"Again, only when Joshua wanted to show me something. I haven't got a clue what's going on around here. His reluctance to divulge what trouble the business was in was a grave concern for me. If I had the money to put into the firm, I think I would have needed to have got my solicitor involved, ensure the contract reflected my concerns."

"Sounds to me that you may have had trust issues with Joshua. Did you?"

"Tell me someone who doesn't when they're considering handing over a vast amount of money and when the owner of that business is coming across as... I suppose *cagey* would be the word."

"I get your point. Has anyone come to the office who has possibly raised your suspicions at all? Say in the last couple of months?"

"I can't think of anyone, not right now." He flicked back his sleeve and peered at his watch. "I'm sorry, I know this isn't an ideal time to end this conversation, but I have a reputation to uphold and I'm never late for an appointment."

Sara smiled and rose from her seat. "Can I leave you my card?"

"Please do. I believe I have a couple of hours spare tomorrow. I could use the time to search his office, see if anything comes to light, or do you advise me against doing that?"

"I have no objection, however, I would prefer it if a member of my team assisted you in the task, if you're agreeable to it?"

"I don't see why not. I have nothing to hide. Maybe we should run it past Joshua's family first. What do you think?"

"I can give Gail a call today and get back to you. I need to see if she was aware of the firm's financial situation."

He sucked in a breath. "Maybe all this will be too soon for her to consider. Please, tread carefully, won't you?"

"Don't worry, I will. Thanks again for seeing us. I'll give you a call before five, how's that?"

"Please do. Good luck with your investigation. I hope you capture the culprit soon. Before you leave, umm... this is purely selfish of me to ask, but you don't think the killer will strike again, do you? Come here? Come after me?"

"I don't think that will be the case; however, it wouldn't hurt to keep your wits about you for the time being."

"I'll do that, thank you, Inspector. I'll show you out. I can collect Mr Atkins at the same time. He's bound to be waiting in reception. He's about as keen on good timekeeping as I am."

"Will it be okay if we had a word with the rest of the staff before we leave?"

"Of course. All I ask is that you question them out of earshot of our clients, if any should drop in."

"I don't have a problem with that, Mr Bates. Do you have another office we can use?"

"Unfortunately not, only Joshua's, and I'd rather you didn't use that out of respect for him. What about the staffroom? Will that suffice?"

"Sounds perfect. Thank you."

He showed them through to the reception area again, collected his client and had a quick word with the receptionist who nodded and walked towards Sara and Carla.

Paula greeted them with a smile that was hard to read. "Mr Bates said that you'd like a word with us before you leave."

"That's right. Separately, if that's okay? He suggested we hold the interviews in the staffroom."

"There's only myself and Maureen to speak with. I'm Paula by the way."

"That's fine, Paula. We won't keep you too long, I promise."

"Shall I go first? I'm at a convenient point in my paperwork. I'm due a break."

"Why not? Care to lead the way?"

"I won't be long, Mo. Hold the fort for me."

"I will," the other woman said, her smile weak and full of uncertainty.

"Right, come with me. It's back in the direction you've just come from, I'm afraid."

"Don't worry."

She led them towards Mr Bates' office again and then veered off to the right. "Sorry, it's a bit of a mess. I keep saying I'll come in over the weekend and decorate it, but I never seem to find the time."

"No need to apologise. Take a seat."

The three of them sat around a teak table which had metal legs that formed a crisscross pattern. Carla removed her notebook from her pocket and placed it on the table.

Sara inhaled a breath and let it seep out slowly then began the interview. "Paula, the last thing we want to do is put you under pressure, today of all days. I take it Mr Bates has made you aware of the situation and reason behind our visit?"

"I haven't spoken to him since you've talked to him, but he did tell us that Gail rang him this morning to share the sad news about Joshua. I'm trying to hold it together, you'll have to forgive me if I break down. We all had a close working relationship here. Knowing that someone has now left us… is hard to handle. No amount of caffeine has helped

51

either. I assure you, we've drunk copious amounts this morning."

"It's only natural to feel the way you do after hearing about the tragic event. If we can put that aside for the moment..."

Paula nodded.

"What we need to find out is the motive behind Joshua's death. At this stage, just like the page in my partner's note-book, we have nothing. We're starting from scratch with no clues or evidence to go on, therefore, if there's anything that has struck you as odd which has occurred at the office in the last couple of months, we'd like to hear about it."

Paula paused to contemplate the question. "I can't really say that anything is coming to mind. He was what I would call a workaholic, here until six, sometimes seven in the evening. Occasionally, he also worked the odd weekend as well. It's Gail who I feel sorry for, she loved him, cherished him."

"Thanks, she's obviously not taken it well at all, but their son, Allan, is there to support her. Gail told us that her husband rang her on his way home from the pub. Is that how he unwound after a long day?"

"Oh, really? That's news to me. I don't think he could have gone that often. If he did, he kept it to himself. Maybe last night was a one-off. Are you saying that he was drunk when he died?"

"We're awaiting the post-mortem results, so I can't tell you one way or the other."

"Poor Gail. If he was drunk, that's not a nice way for her to remember him, is it?"

"Like I said, I'm not going to make any judgements on that at this point. What about clients? Has he had any prob-lems with anyone lately? Perhaps someone has lost their temper with him, anything along those lines?"

Again, Gail paused for a beat. "I don't think so. I'm sure something like that would have come to mind quickly, wouldn't it?"

"I guess you're right. Okay, I think that's all then. Would it be possible to speak with Maureen now?"

Gail shot out of her chair and tipped it back in her haste to leave the room. Flustered, she righted it and said, "Oh yes, of course. I'll send her in. I think she'll tell you the same. I'd be very surprised if she didn't."

"We'll see." Pushing her luck before the woman had a chance to reach the door, Sara said, "Did you know the firm is struggling financially?"

Paula stood frozen to the spot and stared at her, wide-eyed. "Is it? That's news to me. Is that the true reason behind Mr Bates not becoming a partner? I know he's banged on about it for years but couldn't quite manage to cobble the funds together."

"We're not sure about that aspect at present, we need to run it past Joshua's family, get their take on things. I just wondered if it was something only Joshua and Mr Bates knew about or if it was common knowledge amongst the staff."

"No, this is the first I'm hearing about any kind of problem. Maybe Maureen knew. You're bound to ask her the same questions, aren't you?"

"We'll see. Thanks for taking the time to speak with us."

"Anything to help."

Paula left the room and closed the door behind her.

"All very strange. Wouldn't the staff get a rough idea if something major like that was going on?" Carla asked.

Sara stretched out the knots in her shoulders and replied, "Hard to tell. Maybe he was deliberately keeping a lid on it in the hope that Bates would change his mind. We'll see what the other secretary has to say."

Maureen knocked on the door and poked her head into the room.

"Hi, come in and take a seat."

The woman's mascara had left a trail down her cheeks that Sara hadn't noticed when they had arrived. Maybe she had broken down once the interviews had begun. Only time would tell.

"Are you all right, Maureen? I realise the news about Joshua must have come as a shock to all of you."

She sniffled and produced a tissue from her sleeve. After dabbing at her eyes and then wiping her nose, she screwed it into a ball and held it in the palm of her right hand. Her gaze never left the table. "I can't believe he's gone. If you must know, I've been sat out there, bawling my eyes out. He was such a good man. We were all very close."

The way Maureen said the final part of her sentence made Sara wonder if this woman was more involved with Joshua than either Paula or Mr Bates.

"How close?" Sara asked, taking a punt.

Maureen passed the tissue from one hand to the other without answering the question until Sara prompted her a second time.

"How close?"

"I... we..."

That was as much as she was prepared to say, leaving Sara to fill in the blanks for her.

"You and Joshua were very close, as in intimate, is that what you're getting at?"

Maureen sobbed and nodded. "Yes," she whispered.

Sara sank back in her chair and nudged Carla with her leg. *At last, we seem to be getting somewhere.* "How long had the affair been going on?"

"Six months. We tried to prevent our feelings getting in the way of our working relationship, but neither one of us

54

had the strength to deny what was a natural course of events from happening."

"How long have you worked here?"

"Three years. I despised him at first. No, maybe that was a tad harsh. Let me rephrase that, I couldn't stand being alone in the same room with him. I think he felt the same way, and then suddenly something changed between us and..."

"And?" Sara prompted gently.

"We tried to deny our feelings for each other, but I suppose we'd both reached a certain stage in our life when we wanted more, to feel wanted again."

"I take it you're married as well, Maureen, is that right?"

"Yes. Sometimes I get the feeling my husband barely knows I exist. He spends most nights at the pub, and his weekends consist of several rounds of golf with his work-mates. I need more than that. In fact, tell me a woman who doesn't."

"And neither Paula nor Mr Bates knew about the affair?"

"No, we were very discreet."

"And did either of your families find out that you were seeing each other?"

"No. We were making plans to be with each other but had only just started talking about that. I loved him and he loved me. We wanted to be together, but the logistics weren't in our favour. Neither one of us could afford to rent a property and keep up the payments on our marital homes. We were in a rut and doing our best to get out of it."

"Can you tell us in what way?"

"Just putting money aside where we could. We never met up outside of work, not really."

"I'm confused. Are you telling me that you conducted your affair here, at the office, and yet you still managed to hide it from the others? Tell us how that worked out."

"I was Joshua's personal secretary. He would call me into

his office at regular intervals to take down notes throughout the day."

I bet he asked you to take down more than that, love. "Ah, I see. So, not to put things crudely here, you entered his office for a quick fumble."

Her cheeks coloured up, and she kept her eyes averted. "We did what we could in the time permitted between clients and without causing suspicion between the others. Please don't make our affair out to be more sordid than that, because I'm telling you, we had deep feelings for each other and were making serious plans to be together."

"Yes, you've already said as much. If you were his personal secretary and you were having an affair with him, did you know that the business was in trouble?"

Her head rose, and her brows knitted together. "What? No, I can't believe that's true, he would have told me. You're lying, you must be."

"Mr Bates was the one who told us this morning. I have no reason to lie to you. Did you ever consider why he couldn't afford a hotel room to be with you? Why your affair was conducted in his office and not elsewhere?"

"No. We both made it clear from the outset that we didn't want our affair to put us in any kind of debt, and as our feelings grew for one another, we agreed to put any extra money we had aside at the end of the month."

It was Sara's turn to frown. "As in a joint account, is that what you're telling us?"

"Yes. He told me he had set up an account with the Halifax, and we put the same amount into it every month for the past six months."

"Same amount each or a repetitive payment on your part?"

Maureen nodded. "I put the same amount in each month and presumed he was doing the same."

The red flag started to wave in Sara's mind. "Did you have access to the account, or did you leave everything to him?"

"No, I trusted him. I transferred the funds to his account, and he placed it in the joint one."

Confused, Sara shook her head. "Seriously, remind me where you work again?"

"I don't understand what you're getting at," Maureen snapped, her eyes blazing.

"You work for an accountancy firm, you're having an affair with your boss, and yet every month you're transferring funds from your account to your boss's account."

"Yes, that's what I said. So?"

"With no consideration as to what would happen if his wife found out? Was it his personal account or a joint one with his wife?"

"No, I'm not that daft. I put the money into his personal account."

"Okay, here's another question for you: why did you think the extra step was necessary?"

"What are you talking about? What extra step?"

"I can't get my head around you not transferring the funds to the Halifax account directly. Why go through Joshua's account only for it to end up in the joint one you set up with him?"

Maureen closed her eyes, and the tears dripped onto her cheek as she shook her head. "I've been an idiot, haven't I?"

"Let's not say that. Why don't we say that Joshua blind-sided you and leave it at that?"

"It amounts to the same thing, that he duped me into thinking I was saving for our future. Are you telling me he's stolen that money from me? Is that what you believe?"

"Without proof, I can't say that's the case at all. What I'll need to do is gain access to the account, if you'll allow me to?"

"I don't know how I can do that. All I know is that an account was set up in both our names."

"Did Joshua ever show you evidence of that? They don't have passbooks these days, but I'm sure the Halifax still send out monthly statements, don't they?" Sara glanced in Carla's direction.

"I think they do, unless you request to go paperless. I don't receive one every month nowadays, but that's the way I prefer it. It doesn't matter, it's a waste of time asking me... because only Joshua had access to the account. Why did I do that?"

"Because you trusted him. Look, I'm not for one second casting any aspersions in his direction yet but, now that you've highlighted the issue, it is something that we're going to need to delve into."

"Shit, this could stir up trouble, couldn't it? Do you think his wife knows? Maybe she got wind of this extra account and..."

"Don't stop there. What are you suggesting?"

"Well, she was the one who said she'd found him. What's to stop her from bumping him off?"

"It's definitely something we'll need to consider along with other elements connected with the affair you were having with Joshua."

Maureen scratched the side of her head. "I don't understand. No, wait, yes, I do. Jesus, are you insinuating that I had something to do with his death? That's absurd, you can't really believe that. I thought the world of him, and I've already told you that we were making plans for the future, our future together. Why on earth would I take it upon myself to kill him? It doesn't make sense." Tears welled up and spilled once more.

Sara wasn't really one for taking much notice of open displays of emotion, not from someone who admitted to having an affair with their boss and the victim of a gruesome crime she was investigating. She wasn't easily fooled, not in the slightest. "It's an avenue we're going to have to explore. Of course, now that you've admitted to having an affair, we're going to have to sound out Gail and your husband, too."

"What? Why? No, I can't believe you would do this to me."

"Do what? There is every chance that people who are being cheated on could be forced to take the law into their own hands and seek out revenge. Do you know where your husband was last night?"

"Yes, he was at the pub with his work colleagues for part of the evening and then came home to be with me from about eight."

"And you're sure about that, are you? What pub did he go to?"

"The Red Sparrow at the end of our road, it's his local. Please, isn't there a way around checking out his alibi without telling him why you want to know? Revealing our affair?"

"Possibly. I can't promise to protect you. I'm not blaming you for having an affair as such, but when investigating a murder case, knowing that the victim was having an extra-marital affair essentially highlights the possibility of a motive."

"No one knew about us. I swear they didn't, so I can't see your logic in revealing the affair to Joshua's wife and my husband."

"I think we'll need to agree to differ there."

Maureen's head dropped and rested on her outstretched arms. Her shoulders jiggled, and the room filled with her sobs. Sara quickly glanced at Carla and rolled her eyes. She was getting bored by this woman's reaction now. However, she needed to push her own suspicions aside to search for the truth. What she couldn't ignore was the fact that this woman had admitted to having an affair with a murder victim. Her mind in turmoil, she waited for Maureen to stop crying before she asked anything further.

"Can I get you a drink?" Sara asked.

Finally, Maureen pulled herself upright and shook her head. "No, I think I'm all right now. This is such a traumatic day for me. I've been out there this morning, having to suppress my true emotions so that Mr Bates and Paula didn't suspect anything."

"Do you know if there is a safe on the premises?"

"Yes, Joshua had one in his office."

"Who knows the combination to it?"

Maureen shrugged. "Only Joshua, that's the way he ran things around here. He liked to be the one person in charge. That's why I was surprised when he told me he had offered Ralph a partnership."

"It sounds to me like you didn't really know what was going on in Joshua's head at times, is that correct?"

Maureen's gaze darted to the left, out of the window overlooking the yard at the back of the property, and she said nothing.

Sara left it a moment or two and then repeated her question.

"Why are you doing this to me?"

"Doing what? I'm carrying out my job. If you'd rather we conducted this interview down at the station, that would suit me better. The choice is yours."

Maureen clasped her hands together and swallowed noisily. "No, I haven't done anything wrong. Why are you determined to treat me like a criminal? Is that what you think? That I killed Joshua? Because I'm telling you now, you're way off the mark, Inspector. No one could have loved that man more than I did."

"Perhaps his wife might like to challenge you on that point. We'll have to see about that, won't we?"

"No, you can't tell her. I fear the news will kill her."

Sara inclined her head. "What makes you think that? Do you know Gail Smith well enough to know what state her health is in?"

A defiance developed in Maureen's eyes. "No, I don't."

"Then why say it?"

"I'm putting myself in her shoes. Wouldn't you, if you found yourself in my position?"

"It's never likely to happen because I love my husband and would never cheat on him. I'm surprised you would consider saying it as well."

"Are you? Why?"

"Because if you wanted to protect Gail, you have a funny way of showing it. Why on earth would you start an affair with her husband to begin with?"

"I don't know. He had such a magnetic personality, lots of people were drawn to him."

"Lots of people, or just women? Are you suggesting he'd had several affairs before yours began?"

"No, nothing like that at all. He loved his wife, he would never have done that to her."

Sara shook her head. "You're confusing me. How could he love his wife and yet talk about leaving her to set up home with you?"

Maureen's feistiness wavered, and she plucked another tissue from her sleeve as the tears developed once more.

Sara refused to go easy on her, sensing this was a ploy the woman often used during an argument she feared she was losing. "Okay, if this is all too much for you, then I think we should make arrangements for you to come to the station, perhaps after you've finished work. Maybe interviewing you elsewhere will prove to be more advantageous to our investigation."

"No. I can't. Why won't you believe me? I know nothing."

"Somehow I'm detecting that isn't exactly true."

"I'm not sure what I've said to make you think I know more than I'm letting on. I'm as much in the dark about what's happened as you are. If you think I'm overreacting, you're wrong. I've just lost the love of my life, how would you expect me to act?"

"The love of your life, and yet we're expected to believe everything you've told us so far. Something doesn't add up to me. Forgive me if you believe I'm hounding you for answers, that's because I am. I won't deny it. And the only reason I'm doing it is to get to the truth of why Joshua Smith is now lying in a fridge at the mortuary. Now, are you going to open up to us or not?"

Maureen shook her head. "I have been open and honest with you. I'm sorry if you don't believe me, but it's the truth. All of this has come as a huge shock to me. But please, do you have to tell Gail and my husband about the affair?"

"We've already covered that point. I'm not going to change my mind on the subject, so no amount of pleading on your part is going to convince me to do otherwise. While we're on the subject, I need to know your husband's details, his name and your address."

Maureen's fists clenched, and she slammed them onto the table. "Why? What good is it going to do now that he's gone?"

"You're totally missing what I'm getting at, and I'm not in the habit of repeating myself. Either you give me the details I need to go forward with this investigation, or I ask Paula and Mr Bates to fill in the gaps."

Maureen inhaled and released a shuddering breath. "You've got me in a corner. I'll tell you, but you're making a huge mistake."

"We'll see about that."

"My husband is Andrew Dobbs, and our address is ten Greenbank Road, over in Holmer. In doing this, you're going to ruin my life, my relationship with my husband, and even put my job here in jeopardy."

"I'm carrying out my job. All we need to do is have a chat with your husband. You did all the rest, starting an affair with your boss. So, if you're wanting someone to blame, I suggest you start by looking in the mirror. I think this interview has come to its conclusion now."

Maureen sat there, staring at her open-mouthed until Sara stood. "Wait, where does this leave me? Are you going to tell Mr Bates about this?"

"We're trusting you to come clean and do the right thing. We've got more important things on our agenda for today."

Maureen covered her face with her hands and sobbed. Sara, as heartless as it may seem, had seen and heard enough. She gestured to Carla that they were leaving.

In the corridor, Carla clutched her arm and whispered, "You were really tough on her. Why?"

"How can you stand there and ask that, Carla? The woman was cheating on her husband and having an affair with the victim. Nothing about that scenario sounds right to me."

Carla hitched up a shoulder and took a step back, allowing Sara to pass.

Paula glanced up from her desk as they walked back into the outer office. "Everything okay? You've been with Maureen quite a while."

"We'll leave Maureen to fill you in when she joins you. She shouldn't be too long; she was a little upset."

"Oh my. I'll go and check on her. I'm feeling a touch raw myself. I think once you're alone you tend to dwell on things a bit more than you would if you're in a room full of people. Sorry, I'm waffling. I'm sure you have plenty to do."

"You're not wrong. Go easy on Maureen."

"Easy on her? I don't understand, why wouldn't I?"

Sara smiled. "She might need a shoulder to cry on and a friendly ear to listen to her when she finally emerges. Thanks for all your help today. We'll be in touch if we need to ask further questions."

"Oh, I see. Okay. Yes, we'll support each other. This has come as a shock to both of us."

Sara and Carla left the premises.

Outside, Sara homed in on the coffee shop across the road. "Come on, it's too early for lunch. I'll treat you to a decent coffee and a piece of cake instead, how's that?"

"Suits me."

Neither of them spoke again until they were sitting at the table, stirring the sugar into their coffees.

"I'm sorry if you think I came on a bit too strong with Maureen. I needed to get to the truth without all the pussyfooting around. You know I don't have time for people who have affairs."

"Doh, that much was obvious. I've never seen you over-react that way before, Sara. What's different about this time?"

Sara picked up her fork and sliced through her piece of carrot cake. "I don't know, something snapped within me. I felt she was holding back about something. Was I wrong?" She popped the forkful in her mouth and savoured the texture of the light sponge.

"Not in the end, but you weren't to know that when you started questioning her. My two cents' worth is that you sat in judgement back there as though you were not only the judge but the jury as well. It's her life. If she wanted to have an affair with her boss, that has nothing to do with us."

"No, I suppose you're right, but it could have a huge

bearing on the investigation. Affairs never end well, not from what I have witnessed over the years."

Carla ate her cake, contemplation evident in her expression.

"Nothing to say in response?" Sara asked.

Carla washed her cake down with a sip of coffee. "What would be the use? Your mind is already made up. All I'm saying is that you allowed your prejudice to show, and that's totally unlike you. Why?"

Sara twisted her cup in her saucer, the noise grating, putting her teeth on edge. "I don't know. Maybe I'm just tired."

"Tired in general? I know it couldn't have been easy dealing with a new partner while I've been off, but I'm back now. If you need to take a few days' break, then do it, Sara."

She laughed. "I can cope. When have you known me to buckle under the stress? No, I meant I put in a full day yesterday only to get a call-out late last night; therefore, I didn't get my eight hours."

Carla's eyes narrowed. "Forgive me if I don't believe you and I think you're talking utter bollocks."

"Whatever, it happens to be the truth. Hey, I've got other things on my mind, too, remember."

"I know, but that's still no excuse for what happened back there. You're normally a professional through and through. As far back as I can recall, you've never let your personal life get in the way of work, so what's changed?"

Sara took a sip from her coffee, enjoying the mellowness of the blend compared to the muck they had on offer back at the station. "Can we drop this? I have my reasons for grilling Maureen the way I did. It has nothing to do with what's going on in my personal life, I assure you. Anyway, it worked, didn't it? She was far more forthcoming at the end of our conversation than she was at the beginning, so I must have done something right."

Carla tutted. "You really don't get it, do you?"

"No, I don't. What are you getting at?"

Carla vehemently shook her head. "Nope, I'm not going there. I swore to myself before leaving the house this morning that I was going to ease myself back into work."

Sara laughed. "Maybe you should think about a change of career if you want an easy life then, partner, because, in case you hadn't noticed, the crime rate is on the rise in the UK."

"I know it is. You don't have to treat me like a new recruit."

"Then tell me what you're getting at. Have the courage of your convictions for a change."

"The last thing I want to do is fall out with you, barely a couple of hours back at work, but here goes... I thought you bullied Maureen into that confession."

Sara's coffee spluttered across the table, earning her the odd look of disgust from the customers all around them. "What the fuck are you on about? I did nothing of the sort."

"I beg to differ. But like I said, I don't want to fall out with you. I think we should leave now before you cause us any further embarrassment."

Sara wiped the table with her napkin. It gave her a chance to find the appropriate words for her response. "You're wrong. I didn't speak to her any differently to the way I interview other people connected with a crime of this magnitude."

Carla groaned. "I've clearly said enough. I'm not looking for an argument. You asked me for my opinion, and I gave it to you."

"There's no denying that, along with a smack around the face." Sara pushed the rest of her cake away and left the coffee shop. Murmurings from the other customers followed her to the door.

She waited outside for Carla to join her, and then they walked back to the car in silence.

Once they were seated inside the vehicle, it was Carla who found her voice first. "I'm sorry."

"For what? Speaking your mind or for calling me a bully?"

"Both."

"You're entitled to speak your mind, it's what I've always encouraged in our relationship, but I draw the line at being called a bully."

"Which is why I apologised. I admit I overstepped the mark."

"On that we agree. So, bearing in mind what Maureen divulged after *I bullied her*, what do you propose we do now?"

Carla tutted, clunked her seat belt in place and folded her arms. "I don't know. I would be inclined to sit on the information for a while, especially with you being so wound up about it."

"I dispute that, I'm not wound up. As far as I can tell, my interview technique gained us the answers we were searching for."

"Whatever," Carla mumbled.

Annoyed by her partner's response, Sara started the car and drove off. At the roundabout, she had a decision to make. Did she turn left to go back to the station or right to question Maureen's husband? After a short deliberation, she turned right and headed for the Dobbs' address.

"What if he's at work?"

"Maybe he still works from home after the pandemic. I'm taking a punt that's the case," Sara admitted.

"And what are you going to say when you get there? You haven't even taken a step back and thought that through, yet."

Sara patted Carla on the knee and said, "Why don't you

let me worry about that? It's not like you to be concerned about how an interview might pan out, so why this time?"

"Because I'm not liking which way this is going. Okay, I'll keep my mouth shut then, if that's what you want."

"I'd prefer it, in this instance. My main focus has to be finding the killer and what their motive was for killing Joshua. What better place to start than with the husband of the woman he was having an affair with?"

"Yes, I get it. I just think… never mind. Just please don't come running to me if it backfires on you."

"I won't."

THE DETACHED HOUSE was situated in the middle of a horseshoe estate just off the main road.

"Nice area," Carla said.

"I'm saying nothing, in case you shoot me down in flames again."

"Now you're just being childish," Carla growled.

"If you say so. Are you up for this? Can we drop the attitude and the conflict that's going on between us, just for the next half an hour?"

"Of course. I have my professional head on, ready to take notes. I hope you find the answers you're seeking."

"So do I. If not, we're going to have to go and see the weeping widow and spoil her day further."

"Crap. I'm kind of wishing I'd stayed in bed this morning."

"If you're looking for a cushy day, maybe you've chosen the wrong career full stop, Carla."

"Maybe I have," her partner agreed.

Her answer shocked Sara to the core. "Seriously? You wouldn't jack it all in, would you?"

"It depends. Maybe sitting at home for three months,

watching mindless TV, has given me the inspiration to seek out a better career opportunity for me."

"Bugger off. I don't believe you. Policing is in your blood just like mine."

"We'll see. I think our luck might be in, there's a Merc sitting on the drive."

Sara turned and grinned. "Trust me, I'm a shit-hot detective, something that has clearly slipped your mind during your period of recuperation."

"Whatever," Carla mumbled and exited the car.

Sara did the same, her stomach churning, despite the impression she was giving Carla.

Sara reached the front door first and rang the bell. A man wearing blue jeans and a thick jumper opened it. He removed his spectacles and smiled.

"Hello, can I help you?"

"Andrew Dobbs?"

"That's right, and you are?"

"DI Sara Ramsey, and this is my partner, DS Carla Jameson. Would it be convenient if we come in and have a chat with you, sir?"

"Oh, right. May I ask what this is about?" His gaze flicked between them.

"We're investigating a major crime in the area, and your name has surfaced in relation to one of the people we've spoken to today."

"What is that supposed to mean?"

"If we could come inside, it would be easier for all concerned."

"As I have nothing to hide, then yes, come in."

Sara sensed that was the case with Mr Dobbs. First impressions were telling her that he wasn't the killing type. *We'll see. Maybe my gut instinct isn't up to scratch on this case.*

He showed them into a warm, cosy lounge. There was a

desk in the alcove in the corner with a computer. The screen was lit as if he'd been working on it when they had arrived. On the other side, logs were aglow in the woodburning stove.

"You have a lovely house, sir," Sara said.

He invited them to take a seat. "I'm sure you haven't come all the way out here to just compliment my house, Inspector. If you could come to the point swiftly, I'm expecting an important call within the next ten minutes or so."

"Of course."

Sara and Carla sat on the leather couch, and he took a seat in the armchair closest to the fire.

"How well do you know Joshua Smith?" Sara asked.

His brow creased. "Joshua? Not very well. I've met him on a couple of occasions. We are talking about my wife's boss here, aren't we?"

"That's correct. Did you get along well with him?"

"I'm not sure I would say that. I really haven't had much to do with him over the years. Why do you ask?"

"Unfortunately, Mr Smith was found murdered last night."

He leaned forward, his eyes widening in shock. "What? Does Maureen know about this?"

"Yes, we've just come from the accountants' office."

He held his palms upright and asked, "I don't understand what you're doing here, it's not like I really knew the man. I've met him about four times from what I can remember. Gosh, it's hard to believe he's no longer with us." He glanced at his watch.

Sara took the hint and ploughed on. "The thing is, whilst questioning the staff at the firm today, something came to light that has spun the investigation off in a different direction."

"Okay, I suppose that's what your job is, to seek out the

clues and evidence. I'm still struggling to understand what this has to do with me. Care to give me a hint?"

"As I said, something came to our attention that would be remiss of us not to follow up on."

"Yes, I heard you the first time."

Sara cleared her throat and said, "Were you aware that Mr Smith and your wife were more than close colleagues?" *Why the fuck did I put it like that?*

"I'm not sure what to make of that question. Are you telling me they were having some kind of affair?"

Sara nodded. The phone rang, and he jumped to his feet to answer it.

"Hi, Tim. Something important has come up that needs my immediate attention. Can I give you a call back in half an hour or so...? Okay, thanks, mate... Yes, I think everything is fine... Speak soon." He returned to his seat and flopped into it. "I can't believe this. Are you sure?"

"Maureen admitted as much."

"I'm struggling to get my head around this. Casting my mind back, I sensed there has been something wrong between us for a little while. Foolishly, I put it down to her going through the menopause, or I stupidly believed the excuse she gave me."

"I'm sorry to hear that."

"How long has it been going on? The affair?"

"She told us around six months. I have to ask, as part of the investigation we're dealing with, if you have an alibi for last night, sir."

He stared at Sara, and then his gaze shifted to Carla. "No way! What are you insinuating? That I had something to do with his death?"

"It's a line of enquiry that we need to follow up, sir."

"What a sodding cheek. First you come here, tell me my wife is having an affair, and then you have the audacity to accuse me of *murdering the bastard*. How? Why? This is all news to me…"

"Then you won't mind telling us where you were last night?"

"I stopped off at the Red Sparrow for a couple of pints until around eight and then came home to be with my wife. The woman who, by the sounds of it, is a complete stranger to me. I thought we had a pleasant evening together, and all the while her mind was probably elsewhere, with *her boss*. Shit, I feel sick. What have I done to deserve this? If she's fallen out of love with me, why didn't she come out and just tell me? Why sleep with someone behind my back and come home to me every night, as if she still cared for me? I'm sorry, I'm not allowing you to speak. To say I'm confounded by what you've just told me, well, I just don't know what to say for the best. I never thought this would ever happen to me. All my friends have gone through similar over the years, and I genuinely never thought that I'd ever be joining the club of 'husbands who have been cheated on'."

"I'm so sorry you've had to hear about the affair like this. I felt it was my responsibility to tell you straight away, so forgive me."

"Forgive you? For what? For revealing the truth or for coming here with the intention of blaming me for killing my wife's lover? I wouldn't know where to begin. I'll tell you something, as soon as you leave this house, I swear I'll be straight up those stairs to pack her bags for her. Because if she thinks she can cuddle up to me in bed again at night, like she has for the past twenty-five years, she's got another think coming. I'm astonished to believe how easy it can be to turn from loving a person to hating them within a matter of seconds. She's deceived me all these months, lied to me when I thought we had a strong, solid marriage. I will never be able to forgive her for making a fool out of me. And I don't care if this goes against me in your eyes, but if that man wasn't already dead, I'd be the first in line to kill him. There, I've said it."

Sara nodded, totally understanding the anger that must be flowing through him. "I won't hold that comment against you. All I ask from you is to take a moment to reflect the life you've had with Maureen up until now. Please don't do anything rash that you're likely to regret a few months down the line."

"It's not going to happen. As a couple, there's no way back for us." He shuddered. "Knowing that she's been intimate with that weasel of a man makes my skin break out in hives. I feel lousy just thinking of them together. I'm not sure how I'm going to get past this. Forgiveness will have no place in my heart, though, I can promise you that." He dipped his chin to his chest and placed his hands over his head. "My God, how does one deal with such deception? When all you perceive as happiness turns out to be a big fat lie?"

"I'm sure in time the pain will lessen. Is there anyone we can call to come and be with you?"

"No. I couldn't cope with the shame. I'm not one for opening up to others... I know you'll find that hard to believe, given what I've just said. I'm a private person. Maybe that's been the problem with Maureen over the years. We've tended to cut ourselves off from our friends and family, existed in our own bubble if you like. People should never do that, not if this is the result. God, this is so difficult for me to get my head around. Every time I close my eyes, all I can see is them together. What an absolute dick I've been."

"Please, you mustn't think that. Let me ask someone to come and be with you."

"I don't want or need anyone, not if the one person I love the most in this world has cheated on me, treated me like this. How the hell am I going to trust anyone ever again?

Sorry, you don't want to hear me ranting, venting my anger. Is there anything else you need to ask or tell me?"

"No, we came here specifically to ask where you were last night, and we're satisfied with the answer you gave us as it corroborates what your wife told us. We can go now, but I'd rather not leave you alone, not when you're in such a state. Are you sure there's no one we can ring for you?"

"No. I'd rather be on my own. I can categorically tell you that I didn't hurt or kill her boss. I know this isn't what you want to hear, but I hope he suffered before the end finally came."

Sara got to her feet, and her partner did the same.

"I can't go into details, but I can tell you that he undoubtedly suffered before he took his final breath."

"Good. I know that sounds heartless, but I have no intention of feeling sorry for the man or for Maureen. I'll show you out." When they reached the front door, he asked, "Did his wife know about them?"

"I don't think so. We've yet to break the news to her. The question is, when? It's a tough call, knowing that she's grieving the loss of her husband."

"Maybe he was doing the dirty with someone else as well as Maureen, have you considered that? Perhaps someone less mild-mannered took it upon themselves to punish him for dipping his wick where it wasn't wanted."

"It's a possibility we need to consider. Thank you for seeing us. Sorry we had to be the ones to drop the bombshell."

"I'd rather know than live a life full of lies."

Sara and Carla both nodded and left the house.

"Jesus, that was a bugger. I'm not sure I could bring myself to go through that all over again with Gail," Sara said once they were back in the car.

"Yeah, I wouldn't bother. I know you always want to do

the right thing for the victims' families, but sometimes that can be more painful than losing the person, if you see what I'm getting at."

"Yeah, you're right. Okay, let's head back to the station, see what the rest of the team have come up with, if anything. We'll put their affair to one side for now and revisit it if we need to in the future."

"That's the wisest thing you've said today." Carla sniggered.

SARA HADN'T BEEN BACK at her desk long when her phone rang. "DI Sara Ramsey, how may I help?"

"Inspector, this is Allan Smith. I want to know how the investigation is going. Do you know who killed my father?"

"Oh, hello, Mr Smith. Sorry, but it's far too soon for me to tell you that. These things take time. The results from the post-mortem haven't even landed on my desk yet."

"Okay, so what do you know? Tell me what you've been doing all morning."

"My job, leading the investigation to the best of my ability. There's no need for you to be concerned. My team are working at full steam on this case, we won't let you down."

"And yet I find you in your office. Tell me, how are you going to find a killer sitting on your arse all day?"

Sara's temper rose instantly, and she had to fight to keep it from seeping into her voice when she responded to his outlandish accusation. "For your information, I've only just returned. My partner and I went out first thing to make enquiries."

"Where?"

"To your father's firm. We wanted to see what the staff could tell us. Ask them if he had any issues with any clients or anything in that vein."

"And what did you learn? I thought my mother asked you to keep us updated."

"She did, and I will. But what I won't be doing is keeping you informed every step of the way during the investigation. No police officer will do that. For one thing, I won't have time to do it. I barely spend time in my office as it is."

"And yet there you are, I repeat, sat on your arse."

"Actually, an interesting detail came to light this morning which I believe warranted further investigation." *Me and my big mouth. When am I going to learn not to let people push my buttons and immediately retaliate?*

"Go on, don't stop there, I have a right to know what's going on. Tell me."

Sara sat there, debating whether now was the right time or not to reveal what she had learnt about his father's affair. The more he pushed... "I'd rather keep that information to myself for now, until I have more details to hand. During an investigation of this nature, as you can imagine, several leads come our way, and each one needs to be thoroughly scrutinised for its authenticity before we can take things further."

"What a load of codswallop that is. There's that old saying, Inspector, that I tend to live by: don't bullshit a bullshitter. If you're not prepared to keep us informed, I'm going to have to consider going to your superiors about this."

"My senior officer is fully aware of the situation, sir. She has faith in my abilities, and my record speaks for itself. As I've stated already, these things take time. Please allow me the time to dot the I's and cross the T's, at least for now."

"What utter tosh. If I find out you're keeping valuable information from us, I'll make your life hell."

"Is that a threat, Mr Smith? Oh, sorry, I should have forewarned you at the start of this conversation, all my phone calls are recorded specifically for that reason."

He mumbled an expletive and tutted down the line. "I

apologise. Surely you can imagine what we're going through here, it's the frustration talking."

"I can totally understand how you both must be feeling. This isn't an ordinary death we're dealing with. Murder can be a complex crime to solve and, again, I'm going to have to ask you to bear with me and my team. We have no inclination to let you down, not when we have an exemplary record to maintain. I'll be in touch, if and when, we come across anything that I feel needs to be shared with you."

"I suppose I need to be grateful to have you working on our case. Please, don't let us down, Inspector."

"I have no intention of doing that, Mr Smith. I'll speak to either you or your mother soon." Sara hung up before he had the chance to say anything else.

She sighed and closed her eyes to contemplate if she had done the right thing or not, keeping Smith in the dark about his father's affair. When she opened them again, she found that Carla had snuck into the room and was seated opposite her.

"What the...? You scared the crap out of me. How long have you been there?"

"A couple of hours. Tut-tut, Inspector Ramsey, since when did you take up sleeping on the job?"

"You're winding me up, at least I hope you are."

"I am. Anything wrong?"

"No, literally just resting my tired eyes and giving my brain a breather. I've just had a frank discussion with Allan Smith."

Carla gasped. "Oh no, you didn't tell him about the affair, did you?"

"You're right, I didn't. Although, I was tempted to reveal all at one stage."

"What did he want?"

"To see if we had any news yet."

"What the fuck? Do these people think that evidence and clues just drop into our laps when we're least expecting them or what?"

"I'm sure that must be the case for some people. Anyway, he threatened to put in a complaint to the DCI. I told him to go ahead but that she would tell him the same thing. It's less than twenty-four hours since his father's body was found, talk about being unreasonable."

"People expect us to have a magic wand stored away that we can whip out and wave now and again. Realism doesn't seem to come into it. Anyway, I've got a bit of news for you that is either going to cheer you up or have you pulling your hair out."

"I can't wait to hear what it is." Sara sat upright and picked up a pen.

"Christine has found something interesting in Smith's bank account."

"The deposits made by Maureen?"

"I was coming to that, they're there as well. No, eighteen months ago, thirty thousand pounds was deposited into his account."

"What? Where did it come from?"

"It was a cash payment."

"Right, and could the bank give any further details on it?"

"I rang them. They said he'd come into some inheritance and the money had been found at the bottom of the wardrobe at his aunt's house."

Sara chewed on her lip. "Hmm... that's an unlikely story if ever I heard one. Shit, that's another dilemma I need to consider."

"I'm not with you."

Sara scratched the side of her face. "Whether to run it past Gail and Allan or not. Shit! I don't know what to do for the best."

"What would you usually do? What's going on? Why are you hesitating so much?"

"I don't know. Gut reaction, I suppose. It doesn't help that the son just threatened me."

Carla bounced forward in her seat. "He did what?"

"In a roundabout way. I called him on it, told him I was recording the conversation."

Carla laughed. "Good thinking. What did the moron say?"

"That if I didn't keep him informed about the investigation he was going to make my life hell."

"What a fucking dickhead."

"You're not wrong. There's something about this case that's clawing at my stomach, but I'm struggling to put my finger on it."

"Let's face it, the more we uncover, the more I'm inclined to agree with you. Something isn't adding up."

"Agreed. Sod it. Let's get over there and have it out with them. Like you rightly said, I wouldn't normally hold back from seeking out the truth. We can't feel sorry for people, whether they're grieving or not. The fact is, we have a killer who we need to track down."

"Quite right. What about the son? Is he on your radar?"

"Definitely, hard to dismiss his anger issues. Come on, let's go into battle with them, shake the tree, see what falls out."

Carla rubbed her hands together. "Yes, and she's back in the room again."

Sara laughed and followed Carla out of the office. She made a beeline for Christine who showed her the relevant bank statement. "Interesting stuff, and he just fed off that money. It didn't last long either, not by the look of things." She cast her eye over the last six months' deposits and instantly spotted Maureen's money going into the account.

"Jesus, he stung her for five hundred quid a month. What a bastard."

"Yep, my thoughts exactly. I'm eager to see where this case is going to lead us," Carla said. She went over to her desk and hitched on her jacket. "I'm ready when you are. Might need to make a quick stop off at the ladies' on the way out."

"Go for it. I don't think I've drunk enough coffee yet for it to affect me." Sara concentrated on the bank statements again. "How far back have you gone, Christine?"

"Two years. Do you want me to keep going?"

"Yes, if you can get hold of five years' worth, I think that would give us much more insight into what we're dealing with here. Also, can you find out if he ever started up a Halifax account? That's supposed to be a joint account with Maureen Dobbs. I'm thinking it was all a ruse on his part, just to get the monthly funds out of her."

"I'll see what I can find out. What a man, eh?"

"Yeah, I never thought I'd hear myself say this about a victim, but the more we're learning about him, the less I like him."

"I agree."

Sara stopped short of sharing her thoughts about whether she thought the victim deserved to die or not. "I'll see you later. Carla should be finished and set to go now. A quick word with you, Craig, before I leave."

"Yes, boss."

Sara approached his desk. "I know we said we weren't going to focus on the cameras on this case, but I've changed my mind. Can you see what you can find for me?"

"Of course. I haven't got around to searching them as yet. I'll get on it now."

"You're a star. Ring me if anything shows up. We shouldn't be too long."

. . .

IT SEEMED strange to be back at the Smiths' house so soon. Sara's stomach was churning like an ice cream paddle, wading its way through a thick caramel sauce.

Allan Smith must have heard the car doors slam. He opened the front door almost immediately. "Do you have some news for us?"

"Let's go inside. I think your mother should be the first to hear what we have to say."

"Oh, you do, do you? I think otherwise. It's my job to protect her now that my father is no longer around to fulfil the role."

"I'm sorry, I don't agree with you. Why don't we see what your mother has to say about the situation?"

His mother appeared in the hallway. "Allan, stop it. Let the officers in. I want to hear what they have to say, it's my right. He was my husband long before he became your father."

He bowed his head in shame and gestured for Sara and Carla to enter the hallway.

"Come through to the lounge," Gail said and led the way.

The four of them made themselves comfortable, well, bar Sara, who sat on the very edge of the sofa. Allan sat on the arm of his mother's chair, just like he had the previous evening when Sara had last visited the couple.

"Well, what do you have to tell us?" Allan demanded.

His tone earned him a stern look from his mother to which he mumbled yet another apology.

"Actually, it's been a busy day for us. We have a couple of things that we need to make you aware of. Neither of them is very pleasant, I'm afraid," Sara warned. She kept her focus on Gail, keen to monitor her reaction to the news once it was delivered.

Allan sighed but said nothing.

His mother gripped his hand with both of hers. "Go on, I think we're ready for what you have to tell us."

"First of all, I'd like to ask if you and your husband ever discussed financial matters, Gail."

She glanced at her son with a perplexed expression. "Umm... now and again, why?"

"Shall we say some anomalies have come to our attention whilst going through your husband's bank account."

"Such as?" Allan asked.

"Can you tell us why there was a cash deposit of thirty thousand pounds made into his account in June twenty twenty-two?"

Gail stared at her son and shook her head. "I've got no idea, this is the first I'm hearing about it. What about you, Allan? Did your father mention anything to you?"

"No, likewise, this is all news to me. Isn't there a paper trail you can follow?"

"Sadly not. Cash deposits are treated differently to transfers from another account. We made enquiries with the bank, and they told us that Joshua said the funds came from an inheritance. That his aunt had kept the money in her wardrobe at home. Doesn't that ring a bell with either of you?"

"Nothing at all," Gail said. "I'm shocked to learn about this. Why would he keep something like that from me?"

Sara paused before she hit them with the second piece of shitty news. She decided to put a different spin on how things had been uncovered that day. "There's more... we also noticed a number of payments going into his account, dating back four months, from a Maureen Dobbs."

"What? That's the woman who works for him, she's his secretary," Gail said, her eyes widening with shock.

"Have you had this out with her?" Allan asked. "This Dobbs woman?"

"Yes. I'm sorry to have to inform you that she told us she was having an affair with your husband."

"What? That's insane. There's no way my father would have cheated on my mother, no frigging way," Allan shouted and rose to his feet. He went over to the fireplace and rested his arm on the oak mantelpiece.

"How long had it been going on?" Gail whispered, her gaze dropping to the carpet in front of her.

"Six months."

"No way. I don't believe a word of it," Allan shouted. He marched across the room and took up his seat next to his mother. He held her hands, but she pulled them out of his grasp. "Mum, don't tell me you had an inkling that this was going on, did you?"

Gail nodded. "He told me a few months ago that he had fallen out of love with me."

"What the fuc...? And you didn't think to run this past me?"

"It was our problem, our marriage. It was no concern of yours, Allan. That might sound a bit harsh, but I believe children should be kept in the dark about such matters. I was hopeful of working things out with him."

"Christ almighty. I thought I knew you two, apparently, I was wrong. What the hell? I can't believe I'm hearing this. How could you do this to me?" He groaned and rushed to the door.

Gail stretched out an arm to stop him, the impact of what was going on written in her features. He barged past, his muttering indecipherable.

"Go, that's it, walk away, just like your father always did when things got too heated for him."

"He didn't. He was always there for you, Mum. How can you sit there and say that?"

"Easily, because it's the truth. Have you not heard a word that has been said here today? Your father was a liar and a cheat. I thought I loved him, once upon a time, but over the past year, admittedly when you haven't been around, he's treated me abysmally. Some days I've felt like an intruder in my own home. I see now, after what the inspector has told us, that he was trying to force me to leave him, probably so that he could move that Dobbs woman in, to fill my shoes and to sleep in my bed."

"He wouldn't have done that to you, *to us*, Mum, he just wouldn't have."

"How do you know that? Did you know he was seeing this other woman?"

"No, I've already told you, I didn't have a clue. Hey, how do we know it's the truth? It's not like we can confront him about his affair, can we? No, because he was fucking murdered last night. Get real, Mum, we're hearing this gossip secondhand. I'm going to drive into town and have it out with Maureen face to face. I want to look her in the eye when she tells me she opened her legs regularly for my father."

"Don't be so bloody crude. Why would she lie when she spoke to the officers earlier?"

"I don't know, Mum, that's why I'm going down there, to have it out with her. I need answers and I'm obviously not going to get them sitting around here."

"Go, do what you want," Gail snapped and turned away from him, giving her son the cold shoulder.

Allan completed his journey and exited the room.

Sara studied Gail, her sympathy gene pricking wildly. "Please forgive me for bringing this devastating news your way, today of all days."

"Nothing to forgive. You have a job to do, Inspector. I should imagine you must go through a gamut of emotions on a daily basis, dealing with the heinous crimes that you're tasked with solving."

"It's never easy. We try to make it as painless as possible for the families involved. To tell you the truth, I was in two minds about informing you of the developments that have come our way so early into the investigation."

"I would think badly of you if you had kept the news from me. Regarding the affair, I had a feeling there was something of that nature going on. Call it gut instinct or women's intuition. Maybe I should have run it past my son before now. I'm not sure he'll be forgiving me anytime soon. I fear what he's going to say or do to Maureen when he lays eyes on her. He shouldn't have left the way he did. She's not to blame for his father's failings, Joshua is. He should have kept it in his trousers. However, like most men, when this woman showed him what he'd been missing out on at home, it was hard for him to say no. That's putting things simply, isn't it?"

"Perhaps. May I ask when you realised there was something wrong with your marriage?"

"I'm not sure exactly, maybe towards the beginning of the year. I asked him outright. He said he was dealing with a lot of pressure at work. I took him at his word and didn't have it in me to force the issue. My health hasn't been the greatest this year, I've had a few scares in one form or another that I'd rather not discuss. Maybe I'm guilty of taking my eye off the ball and not giving either my marriage or my husband the attention they deserved."

"You can't blame yourself. What about the lump sum of money? Can you cast your mind back and recall any conversations that took place between you and your husband around that time?"

"I've been sitting here trying to do that, in between

arguing with my son, and no, nothing is coming to mind. Thirty thousand, wasn't it?"

Sara nodded. "That's right. I would class it as a larger-than-usual deposit, which would raise a few eyebrows down at the bank."

"Did it cause any suspicion? Money laundering, that type of thing? Isn't that what you call it?"

"Yes, that's right. I think the bank took your husband's word on how the money had come his way and chose not to take it further. Has he banked with them a long time?"

"Yes, around thirty years. He hated the thought of switching banks when times got bad. I really don't know what else to say about it, Inspector."

"Okay, we'll try and do some more digging."

The front door slammed, and Gail jumped out of her seat. She ran to the window and banged on the glass. "No, Allan, don't go. I need you."

Sara raced over to the window, arriving there just in time to see a black car speed out of the close. "Come and sit down, there's nothing you can do about it now." She guided Gail back to her seat. The distraught woman had been through enough in the past twenty-four hours, without her selfish son adding to her miseries.

Gail sat and pulled the cushion onto her lap and continued to cry.

"I'll make you a drink, a nice cup of tea, yes?" Sara said.

"If you wouldn't mind, strong and sweet, two sugars. I don't usually have it that way, but I think it's helping me to combat the shock.

Sara smiled and left the room. Once she'd filled the kettle, she rang Ralph Bates. He was in a meeting, but Maureen answered the phone.

"I have to tell you that Allan Smith is on his way to see

you. Can you make up an excuse and leave the office for the day?"

"What? Oh no, this is the last thing I wanted or needed. I take it you told him the news."

"I had to. I'm conducting a murder investigation, and any evidence of this nature is regarded as vital and needs to be shared."

"I'll collect my bag and go home."

"Ah, you might need to reconsider that option. I would advise going somewhere neutral, a café or similar venue. Just do it quickly, he'll be there soon."

"Are you telling me you've told my husband?"

"I had to, yes."

Maureen whimpered. "What the hell for?"

"I'm not about to justify my actions, Maureen, and I've already explained that to you. I needn't have rung you to prewarn you to be cautious, it's up to you what you do with the information. I'm here dealing with the fallout with Gail."

"I'm sorry. Pass on my condolences to her."

"I won't, I'm sorry. I should imagine that's the last thing she'll want to hear. Just take care of yourself and get out of there before…"

"Before what? Is he coming here to kill me, is that what you think?"

"Hardly, however, he was extremely angry when he left." The kettle switched off. "I have to go now. Take care."

"That's it! You destroy what was left of my life and your parting words are 'take care'."

"I think you'll find your actions did that, not me." Sara hung up. She completed making the cup of tea for Gail with questions ripping through her mind, the main one being whether she had done the right thing or not, coming here today, sharing the news about Joshua's infidelity. She'd never had to query her decision-making during an investigation before, well, not since her rookie days in the Force, so why now? Why was this case really getting to her, affecting her judgement? Or was it?

Carla came into the kitchen. "Sara, are you all right?"

"Truthfully, I'm not sure. I'm wondering if I've screwed up or not."

Carla took a step towards her and placed her hands on Sara's forearms. "You can get that out of your head. You've done nothing wrong here, you're following the clues, that's all. If the affair turns out to be a significant angle to investigate then you've made the right call."

"And if it's not? Then what? How many more lives are going to be destroyed before we can put this case to bed?"

"Again, that's down to the people involved, not you. Come on, you're going to need to pull yourself together, Gail will be wondering where we are."

Sara flicked out her arms and smiled. "Thanks, partner. I'm glad you're back beside me once more."

"I'm always beside you whether I'm on or off duty, just remember that. You're going to have to put your personal life aside for now. You've done it before, you can do it again."

"You're right. You will tell me if you think I'm overstepping the mark, won't you?"

"Don't worry, I will. And for the record, I don't think you've put a foot wrong so far, you're daft to think otherwise."

Sara smiled and shrugged. "Not sure what's got into me today, but I'm glad you're here to keep me on the straight and narrow."

They shared a brief hug then returned to the lounge to check on Gail.

"Here you go. How are you feeling now?" Sara handed Gail her mug of tea.

"Confused, angry, resentful. About everything, not just

what you've told me today—that's going to take me a while to get my head around. I'm scared more than anything, I've never seen my son so angry."

"It's okay, you're entitled to have conflicting emotions running through you. I've contacted the office and warned them that Allan is on his way. I've advised Maureen to go elsewhere."

"I'm glad. I was about to suggest the same. It's better for her to avoid any conflict, they're both going to be emotionally wrought right now. Is there anything else you need from me, Inspector? Only I think I have one of my migraines coming on, and if I don't get to bed early enough, I know it's going to cripple me within an hour or two."

"No, we'll get out of your hair. Is there anything you need us to do before we leave?"

"I don't think so. You've been very kind throughout. I'm glad you're in charge of this investigation. I'll take my tea with me."

The three of them left the lounge and parted at the front door.

"We'll be in touch in a few days. I hope you feel better soon, Gail."

"Yes, yes, see yourselves out and close the door behind you, if you would."

CHAPTER 3

"*I* can't, not tonight, fellas. I promised my wife I would go straight home. It's our wedding anniversary, and she's a bit narked I chose to come here tonight as it is."

"Happy anniversary, mate. We'll help you celebrate next week then. I hope she likes the tray you made her," Darren said as the group walked towards the cars.

"She's been nagging me to get her one for ages, this will have to do. Have fun, guys. See you next week."

The group of classmates went one way, and Harry went the other. He pressed the key fob, and the doors of his car clunked open. He put the tray he'd made at his evening woodworking class into the boot and shut the door. He whistled merrily and slipped behind the steering wheel, reaching for the door to find a man standing there. "What the hell do you want?"

"A little chat before you head home for the evening."

"We've got nothing to talk about. I said my piece to you the other day, along with the others. We've all agreed you're a menace to society. Intent on making our lives miserable because you're a selfish bastard."

The man laughed. "I couldn't have put it better myself. At the end of the day, *mate*, I couldn't give a fuck what you cretins think of me."

"I'm not your *mate*. I couldn't think of anything worse than being linked to you and what you stand for."

"Is that right? Maybe you and your cohorts are envious of the cash I'm pulling in."

"We're not, far from it. You'll get your comeuppance one of these days, and we'll all be there applauding the authorities when they finally catch up with you. Karma can be a bitch, so I'm told."

The next thing Harry knew he was being wrenched from the car, and he ended up on the ground at the man's feet. Fear his dominant emotion. He hated everything about this man. He tried to get to his feet, but his attacker forced him down again.

"There are too many people around here for you to carry out your intentions. You'd be a fool to do anything you're going to regret."

"Stop with the name-calling, as usual. You're getting on my nerves. You and the others are going to get what's coming to you. I should have done this long ago; you've caused me a mountain of anxiety in the past six months. Sent different departments my way because of your whinging and complaining all the time. Well, I've had enough of it and I'm going to punish the lot of you."

Harry tried to get to his feet again, but the man stamped on his chest, the weight of his working boots adding to the impact which took his breath away. The man didn't hold back, he pummelled him with his fists, leaving him bloody and dazed.

Harry pleaded with him to stop. "Don't do this. We'll stop,

I'll have a word with the others. If that's what it'll take for you to leave us alone."

"Words are cheap. I need actions, and you've all shown your true colours in that department over the years. The time has come to seek my revenge."

Two more punches, and Harry lost consciousness.

He woke up a little while later, surrounded by darkness. It took him a while to realise that his hands had been tied and there was tape over his mouth, but where was he? It felt like he was inside something that was moving. As the fog cleared in his brain and the smell of oil reached his nostrils, he managed to work out that he was in the boot of a car. He searched the area behind him and recognised something he was lying on—the tray he had made during the evening at night school—which meant he was in the back of his own vehicle. He lay there, wondering where his journey would end and what his fate was going to be. Judging by what his attacker had put him through already, he feared the worst. After saying a silent prayer, he lay there and listened. After a few more seconds, the road turned bumpy.

Where the hell is he taking me? Down a country road? A farm track? Probably, knowing him. Shit, why did I have to get involved with the others? We thought we'd be okay, safety in numbers and all that. Yeah, look where that got me. Jesus, what's going to happen to me? The intent in his eyes was telling when he hit me and knocked me out. Stop thinking, it's not going to get me anywhere.

The car turned sharply, and the road beneath him became smooth once more, which caused him to become even more confused. Then the car stopped. Footsteps sounded on the gravel, and then the boot sprang open. He was yanked from the car and made to walk several feet. His eyes took a while to adjust to the darkness, then his vision cleared enough to see that he was being led towards an area where the trunk of a tree crossed the path in front of them. He didn't recognise this area at all and yet he'd lived in Hereford his whole life, thought he knew every inch of it like the back of his hand. He was wrong.

"What are you going to do to me?" Harry said, his words muffled by the tape.

"And you expect me to understand what you're saying? Think on, Brown. And no, I won't remove the tape. You're going to have to suffer in silence instead."

Harry was forced to sit on the log. The man threw the bag he was carrying on the ground and unzipped it. Harry's mouth dried up, and his eyes widened as tool after tool was removed from the bag. While the man was distracted, Harry did his best to get to his feet with the intention of making a run for it, but his ageing body let him down.

"Sit there and accept your fate, tosser. The more you try to avoid the inevitable, the worse your punishment is going to be. Listen to me," the man shouted, leaning down and spitting in Harry's face as he spoke. "You need to accept what's coming to you. You and your pals have been at me for months now. I've reached the end of my tether, and this is me lashing out. Ending it all. Tonight will be your last. I'm going to take pleasure in killing you, as much pleasure as I got last night when I killed your mate, Joshua. He received a very satisfactory ending, from my point of view anyway." He tipped his head back and laughed.

"No, please. What are you talking about? What about my family?" His words were again silenced by the tape. What was the use in continuing to waste his breath?

"Accept it and it'll all be over soon enough. If you kick up a fuss, it's only going to prolong your agony. The choice is yours, old man."

He raised the knife above his head. Harry's gaze followed the movement, and he closed his eyes once the blade began its descent. The pain erupted in his stomach before the man

93

struck again and again. The smell of blood lingered, and the pain increased, but he refused to open his eyes and give the man the satisfaction of witnessing the fear within them. He did as instructed, accepted his fate with courage instead of fear flowing through his veins.

With every blow he dished out, the man shouted expletives and bombarded him with vile names that Harry had never heard before. Not long after the attack had begun, Harry's power to resist crumbled. He fell sideways onto the trunk, his breath coming in fits and starts, hampered by the tape stretched across his mouth. His attacker knew his ending would be swift, and Harry got the impression he was regretting not being able to extend Harry's torture.

His heart rate slowed; he could sense the end was near now. Finally, he opened his eyes to see the angry man collecting more tools from the bag. Harry's eyes flickered shut and this time remained closed as his body shut down... for good.

CHAPTER 4

*S*ara and Carla were in a race to get to the scene, and
the traffic was a nightmare to get through at this
time of the day. Sara had received the call at seven that
morning. Mark was in a mood with her when she'd left the
house, nothing new there. She had picked Carla up from the
police station car park and immediately got on the road
again to the location where they knew Lorraine would be
waiting for them.

"Get out of the sodding way, will you? What's the point in
us using the blues and twos if no one takes a blind bit of
notice of them?"

"Arseholes, the lot of them. Makes you wonder if they'd
react the same way if one of their family members was in
trouble."

"It does. I don't think I've been out this way before, not to
the actual location, Lower Lyde. What's it like?"

"Usually a nice little community. No crime from what I
can recall. That's probably why you've never visited it
before."

The traffic eased after several more fraught minutes. Sara

turned off the sirens and lights once they were on the main route out of the city. "Thank God for that, it was doing my head in. I hate turning up at a scene wound up."

"No shit, Sherlock." Carla laughed.

"Don't take the mick. How are you feeling after your first full day back at work yesterday?"

"Des spoilt me last night. We had a takeaway, and I was tucked up in bed by eight-thirty, exhausted."

"And today?"

"A bit weary but not too bad. I'll give you the nod if I need forty winks during the day."

"You should have brought your pillow and quilt with you; I could have made up a bed for you on the back seat."

"You're all heart. Thanks for caring, Sara, you're the best boss around, I don't care what the others say about you."

Her derisory comment earned Carla a dig in the leg.

Sara pulled up at the crime scene around ten minutes later. They got suited and booted then went in search of Lorraine who was surveying the area a few feet off the track, at the edge of the woods.

"Hey, how's it going?" Sara asked.

"I have two words for you. Actually, it's three."

"Go on, let's have them," Sara said, although after viewing the victim she had an idea what Lorraine was about to say.

"Same modus operandi."

"Shit, and yet the location is miles from the first murder, not that it matters. Do we know when he was killed?"

"Rough estimate, I would say between nine and ten last night."

"Who found him?"

"The usual dog walker in a place like this. He's over there, in the back of the squad car with his pampered pooch."

"How do you know it's pampered?" Sara asked, intrigued.

"I don't need to have a detective badge, I just followed the clues. The dog had one of the thickest coats I've ever seen, and the man gave him dozens of treats while I had a two-minute conversation with him."

"Okay, what type of dog?"

"A yapper. Why?"

"I just like to receive all the facts before I go headlong into a situation."

Lorraine jabbed a thumb in Sara's direction. "Is she for real?"

"I'm keeping out of it." Carla chuckled.

"Very wise, I wouldn't want you to be accused of taking sides. Anyway, getting back to business, I would suggest you check your missing persons records, see what shows up. My take is the man was driven out here by the killer, tortured at length on this trunk and left here with the intention of the body being found quickly. Oh, and in case you hadn't noticed, his car was set on fire, too. Not very well, granted, because it burnt out not long after it was started. I'm presuming that was due to the weather conditions last night. Gusts of winds up to ninety miles an hour, accompanied by torrential rain, which yes, has caused us a lot of problems."

"Damn, at what time did the weather change last night?"

"Around my way the rain hit at about ten-fifteen."

"I was in bed," Carla added.

"I went at around ten-thirty, and it was still dry where I live. Carla, why don't you ring the station? See if the reg of the car is intact first and get them to run it through the system."

Carla went back to the car and placed the call.

Sara covered her boots with the plastic shoes and took a few steps to inspect the victim. "Can I get closer?"

"Go for it. His eyes were found in a bag close to his car, his ears were placed under that branch on the right, and his tongue is missing."

"What the fuck is the killer up to? Why treat them this way? One question... actually, I have dozens of them, but my main one is, were these injuries carried out after the victim had passed away?"

"Some were, the worse ones, but he was stabbed repeatedly first. My thoughts are that he died from those wounds, otherwise the killer would have had a struggle on his hands getting the victim to lie there while he sewed up his mouth and eyes."

"Doh, I should have considered that before I asked. Sorry, my mind was racing and didn't stop to analyse things properly."

"You're forgiven. Now, I'm going to have to get on. You know me, I hate leaving a victim in situ for too long. Why don't you have a chat with the man who found him? I think he's eager to get on his way."

"I'll do that. What's his name?"

"Bert Watkins."

Sara nodded and set off towards the patrol car parked up by the cordon. She opened the back door and was immediately attacked by the snarling Yorkie. "Sorry, I should have knocked first. Mr Watkins, is it?"

"That's right. And you are?"

Sara flashed her ID. "I'm DI Sara Ramsey, the SIO on the investigation."

"I take it that means that you're the one in charge. What a terrible thing to stumble across this morning. How I managed to prevent myself being sick is beyond me. Scared the crap out of me, finding him out here in that state."

"So sorry you had to witness such a gruesome sight. I wonder, did you see anyone else hanging around when you showed up?"

"No, there was only his car here, no one else in the area

either. There's no way he could have done that to himself, is there? So, what are we talking about here, murder?"

"That's what our initial assessment is leading us to believe. Do you recognise the victim? Either him or his car perhaps?"

"No, never seen him before. I'm sorry, I don't drive so I have very little interest in cars."

"That's okay. What time did you find the body?"

"Around six-thirty this morning. I had to walk back to the main road to pick up a good reception on my phone before I rang nine-nine-nine. They told me to return to the location and someone would be with me straight away. A patrol car beat me to it; they were on the ball getting here."

"I'm glad they arrived promptly. Did you see anyone else hanging around?"

"No, I come down here early every day, whatever the weather, summer and winter. Tiggy loves it down here, it's one of his favourite walks."

"When you've been here recently, have you seen anyone acting suspiciously?"

"I can't say I have. I don't tend to see many people down here, not at that time of the morning."

"Okay. Thanks for waiting around to see me. We're going to need to take a statement from you. Can you give your address to the constable? We'll get that arranged ASAP."

"Of course. I'll do anything to help you find the person who did this. Appalling, it is, for one human being to treat another in this way. I keep seeing it on the news, you know, that crimes are getting worse around the country. Never thought I'd see the likes of that kind of thing, not here in Hereford. I bet I'll have nightmares about this discovery for blooming years to come."

"The only advice I can give you is to try not to think

about what you've witnessed today. Block it out of your memory, if you can."

"I reckon that's going to be easier said than done. I must get going. Do you want my details?"

"Yes. Hold on." Sara took a step back. "Constable, can you get down Mr Watkins' details for me and pass them on to the desk sergeant when you return to the station? Ask him to arrange taking a statement from the gentleman."

"I'll do that, ma'am."

"All sorted. We won't keep you longer than is necessary. Thanks again for doing the right thing and contacting the police." Sara smiled and walked back towards the crime scene.

Carla joined her halfway. "The victim's name is Harry Brown. He lives at the Crosslands estate out at Withington."

"Brilliant, that was quick. Did you check if he'd been reported missing?"

"Yep, at eleven last night by his wife, Alice."

Sara sighed. "Great. We'd better get over there and break the news to the family. I just want to have a quick word with Lorraine first."

"Want me to wait in the car?"

"If you want to. I won't be long."

Lorraine turned, hearing her approach. "Poor bugger, right? He was a snivelling wreck when I showed up."

"He's not too bad now. Bloody dog nearly had my hand off, though."

Lorraine laughed. "You should have showed up with a bagful of treats."

"Silly me. Hey, you owe me some PM results from yesterday. When can I expect them?"

"What the fuck? I can't be in two places at once. You're going to have to be patient. I'll see if I can send them both to you tomorrow, unless... the killer strikes again."

"Crap, don't say that. With two murders to solve, we've got enough to deal with. I'm not sure I can cope with having yet another serial killer on our patch."

Lorraine shrugged. "It's the sign of the times. I blame... yeah, I'm not going there, I think we've had this conversation on more than one occasion over the years."

"I believe we have. I'm heading over to inform the victim's wife, wish me luck."

"I think we're both going to need a lot of luck with this investigation, judging by the killer's MO."

"I hope you're wrong. Let me know if you find any evidence lying around."

"You'll be the first to know."

CARLA JOINED Sara at the front door of the small, detached house on the edge of the estate. A tractor had held them up, blocking the entrance, and the farmer had taken a fair bit of persuading to move. Carla had jumped out of the car, flashed her ID at the man, who'd apologised and tipped his cap at her, then he made out he hadn't seen them trying to enter the estate.

"Jumped-up fucker. You could tell he hated speaking to a female officer," Carla complained under her breath.

Sara rang the bell. "Takes all sorts to make up this world of ours. Chauvinistic pigs like that must make up about forty percent."

Carla laughed. "God, I hope not. If it's true, that's a massive proportion."

Sara grinned. "Did I tell you maths was my worst subject at school?"

The door opened, putting an end to their conversation.

"Hello, Mrs Brown?"

The woman, who was in her mid-fifties, peered over her shoulder and called out, "Emily, I think it's the police."

A younger woman in her early thirties appeared beside Mrs Brown. "Are you?"

"Yes, that's right. I'm DI Sara Ramsey, and this is my partner, DS Carla Jameson. Would it be possible for us to come in and have a chat with you?"

"Have you found him? My father?"

"Let them in," Mrs Brown said. "Stop hounding them on the doorstep. I don't want the neighbours hearing what they have to say."

"I asked a simple question, Mum, that's all. You'd better come in."

Mrs Brown and her daughter led them into a large, open-plan kitchen-cum-living room at the rear of the property, which overlooked a stunning back garden full of colour, despite the time of year.

"Can we offer you a drink?" Mrs Brown asked. She sat on one of the stools at the kitchen island and invited Sara and Carla to do the same.

"Not for us, thank you," Sara replied. She inhaled a breath to calm her racing pulse. This was still one of the worst tasks her job involved. The more she did it, the worst it got.

"Well? Have you found him?" Emily said in a panicked tone.

"I'm sorry to have to inform you that we believe Mr Brown's body was found earlier this morning."

Sara watched the colour drain from Mrs Brown's face.

Her daughter instantly burst into tears. "No, this can't be right, not my father, he can't be dead."

Her mother reached for her hand and gathered it in her own. Emily hugged her mother, and her crying turned into sobbing. Mrs Brown gave Sara the impression that she was stunned by the news but adamant she was going to hold it together for the sake of her daughter.

"Where? Did he have an accident?" Mrs Brown asked.

"In a remote spot, near the woods, out at Lower Lyde," Sara replied.

The two women stared at each other.

"Why there?" Emily said. "Do we know anyone who lives out that way, Mum?"

"I was about to ask you the same, darling. I can't think of anyone, no one at all. Not unless someone who your father knows has recently moved out that way, and he forgot to tell me."

Sara raised a hand. "He was found in a remote area, on the edge of the woods," Sara felt the need to repeat.

"Oh, I see. What was he doing there?" Mrs Brown asked, her eyes narrowing.

"Shit! Are you telling us he was with another woman?" Emily whispered.

"No, no, not at all. It was nothing like that," Sara was quick to respond. "What I need to tell you is, your father died in suspicious circumstances." *Christ, I'm making hard work of this.*

"What do you mean, suspicious?" Mrs Brown asked, her brow wrinkling in confusion. "Are you telling us that my husband was up to no good? Breaking the law in some way which ultimately caused his death?"

"No, nothing along those lines, I can assure you. We believe your husband was deliberately driven out to a spot and killed by someone."

Mrs Brown slapped her hands to her cheeks and gasped. "No, this can't be true. Who? Have you got the person who did this? Tell me you've got them."

"Unfortunately not. There was no one at the scene when our colleagues showed up, only the witness, the man who placed the call to alert us after finding Mr Brown's body. Can you tell us when he went missing?"

"Last night. He was at the college. He's just started attending a woodworking class in the evening. He was looking forward to going. Been there for a few weeks now and told me he was going to make me something special last night that I've wanted for a while... yesterday was our wedding anniversary. I spent all evening wondering what the surprise would be, but he never came home. I didn't know who to ring. I didn't start to panic until about ten-thirty. I thought he might have gone to the pub after the class with some of the people on the course. That's unlike him, he's not usually one for drinking a lot and he had health issues."

"He did? Can you tell us what they were?"

Carla removed her notebook from her pocket and scribbled down the information.

"Yes, he had heart problems. He had a triple heart bypass two years ago. I was fed up having him under my feet day and night, so I encouraged him to sign up for evening classes. This is his second course he's taken at the college."

"How long has he been attending the college?"

"This time only a couple of weeks. The last course he did was for poetry. He enjoyed that but wanted to do something more creative with his hands. We checked out all the courses available, and Emily and I suggested he should take up woodworking. He was enjoying it, too, and had made a few friends, something he failed to do on the poetry course. I can't believe he's gone. Why? Why would someone want to bloody kill him? He had a lot of friends and did his very best to help people when he could."

"Has he had any kind of bother lately? At work or maybe with a neighbour?"

"He didn't work, he was forced to retire early because of his heart problems. He used to work for British Rail as a driver. Thankfully, he retired with a decent pension behind him. He was only sixty-two when he had his heart operation. I'm trying to think if he'd fallen out with anyone, and nothing is coming to mind. Emily, can you suggest anything?"

"The only hassle he's had in the last couple of years is with the farm next door. He's had to report the farmer to the Environmental Health because of noise pollution problems."

Sara's interest piqued; she was aware of what they'd had to contend with when they'd drawn up. "I see. And has the issue been sorted out?"

Mother and daughter stared at each other and shrugged.

"Some days we think so and others not. It seems every time we complain and the EH have a word with Sanderson, he does his best to quiet things down a bit, but within days the noise appears to get worse, far worse than it ever was before. We gave up complaining a few months ago."

"How bad did things get?"

"Very bad. The tractors would start working at four in the morning. We think he's recently changed the way he farms. He erected quite a few barns and now keeps the cattle inside; they're never allowed to graze in the fields. I don't call that farming, it can't be right to keep beasts like that inside day and night, squashed into tiny barns. We were told by EH that he has between three and six hundred cows in the barns at any one time. Can you imagine the stench that produces as well? We've had all that to contend with over the years. But like I said, things have died down lately. It all proved too much for some of our neighbours, they sold up and left as soon as the property market picked up. That was never on the cards for us, we love this house and the area we live in."

"How long has the farm been there? Is it new?"

"No, I know it was there before the estate was built. I just get the impression that the farmer does everything he can to make our lives unbearable at times. It comes in fits and spurts, though, it's not all the time."

"And you say you're in touch with the Environmental Health about the problem? Who are you dealing with there?"

"What's his name again, Emily? I've forgotten, my memory isn't what it used to be."

"I can check my emails. Hang on." Emily opened up her phone and scrolled through it. "Here we are, it's Daniel Fitt. I've never really liked him. He left his office and visited us once. Smiled at us all through the conversation. He came across as being very false. Dad couldn't see it, though. He thought he had good intentions and was going to do all he could for us."

"But you didn't get that impression, Emily?"

"No, totally the opposite, in fact. A yes-man who never acted upon the information given to him."

"And have you had any issues with the farmer lately?"

"Now and again. We've accepted the problem for what it is, a pain in the arse that we have to live with because the authorities have no intention of sorting the problem out. I think a couple of neighbours have been in touch with the police a few times."

Sara inclined her head. "Do you know why?"

"Sanderson has threatened them. He's never come out and blatantly threatened us, so I'm not sure what to believe."

"We'll check into it. We had a problem getting on the estate this morning because there was a tractor blocking the entrance."

"Yep, I'm not surprised. He does that type of thing period-ically, just to get a rise out of people."

"Interesting. Okay, it's a lead we're going to follow up. Can you think of anything else we should look into?"

"I can't, no," Emily said. "What about you, Mum?"

Mrs Brown shook her head and then wiped her tears on

the sleeve of her jumper until Emily passed her a tissue from the box on the worktop. "Thank you. No, nothing else. Can you tell us how he died? What injuries he sustained?"

"I think you're better off not knowing. My advice would be to remember him the way he was."

"That's awful. I'll be sitting here, thinking the worst all day now. When can we see him? Will you need us to make a formal identification?"

"After the post-mortem has been carried out. I'll pass on your details to the pathologist. She'll give you a call once she's completed the PM."

"It must be bad if a PM is required," Emily mumbled.

"Not necessarily," Sara corrected her. "It's law when a suspicious death has been confirmed."

"Okay. What happens now? With the investigation?" Emily asked.

"We'll head over to the college, see if anything untoward happened during the class last night or afterwards, perhaps in the car park. We'll also make enquiries into the farmer next door."

"And what about the funeral? Can we start planning that yet?"

"No, you'll need to hold fire for the moment, until the pathologist is ready to release your father's body."

"There's such a lot to take in, I'm not sure if I'm going to be able to cope," Mrs Brown said, fresh tears trickling onto her colourless cheeks.

"Oh, Mum, don't worry, I'm here. We'll get through this together. You're never alone with me around."

"I know, dear. I'm thankful you're here with me. Lord knows what I would have said to the officers if you hadn't been by my side. I'm traumatised. I have a vile image of him being attacked lodged in my mind."

"I'm so sorry," Sara apologised. "There's no easy way of

telling the victim's family that their loved one has passed and the circumstances behind their death."

"We appreciate how you told us today, no complaints on my part. Do you think you'll capture the person who… killed Harry?"

"We're confident we will, but we can't put a time limit on these things. Therefore, I'm going to have to ask you to bear with us."

"I can understand that if you don't have any evidence to go on. I watch a lot of true crime shows on TV, so know a bit about how the police deal with an investigation. Saying that, most of the programmes I see are from America. I'm assuming they do things differently over there?"

"Certain things they do, although the procedures are basically the same. Over the years, we've incorporated many aspects of the way the Americans conduct their investigation; however, we always fall short of telling them that." Sara smiled.

"Quite right, too. I'm happy you're dealing with our case, Inspector, you have a kind nature that I find very reassuring."

Sara blushed. "Thank you. I do my best to always go the extra mile for the victim's family. No one wants a killer roaming the streets of Hereford for long. So, my team and I give it our all when a new investigation drops on my desk. Don't worry, you're in safe hands. We won't let you down."

"I hope not. My husband deserves to have the best officers on his case. Please, you don't have to stay with us, not when you have leads to chase up."

Sara smiled. "As long as you're sure. Is there anyone we can call to come and sit with you both?"

"No, we have each other. My daughter and I are very close, we all were."

Sara and Carla jumped off their stools, and Emily showed them to the front door.

Sara shook her hand. "We'll do our very best for you and your mother, I promise."

"I believe you. Thank you. Just catch this person quickly. There was no reason on this earth why my father should have been hunted down and killed, if that's what happened."

"Leave it with us. We'll be in touch soon."

They left the house and made their way back to the car.

"I'm going to have a quick look around the farm, from a distance," Sara said.

"Aren't you going to question the farmer?" Carla asked, sounding surprised.

"Not until we have all the facts to hand. I want to see what EH has to say about the complaints first. Maybe I should have asked Emily to forward me the emails the family have sent to EH over the years."

"It's not too late, I could nip back and ask."

"You do that. I'll have a wander over there, along the perimeter, have a butcher's and a listen to what's going on."

Carla trotted back to the house, and Sara followed the road around to the edge of the estate. There, she stood on tiptoe and observed what was going on in the farmyard. The same tractor that had blocked the entrance when they'd arrived was moving bales of straw from one side of the yard to the other. Sara could see lots of young cows squashed into one of the barns, and her heart squeezed at their plight.

Is this the level that farming has descended to these days? Breeding cattle to live in barns before they're sent off to the slaughterhouse, not allowing them out into the fields as nature intended? Or is that naïve of me to think that way? I need to do some research into this before I take things further.

The tractor stopped, and the farmer stared at her. Sara smiled and waved at him, but his eyes formed tiny slits, unnerving her. Sara accepted defeat graciously and made her way back to the car. Carla joined her a few minutes later with a handful of papers.

"I've got all the correspondences with EH."

"Good, you can deal with that when we get back to the station. First, I need to drop by the college."

"How did you get on?"

"The farmer caught me looking over the fence and didn't seem too happy. What I saw was heartbreaking. Before I cast aspersions, I need to do some extra research on how the new farming system he's adopted works. From what I can tell, the cows are all squashed into barns until they're ready to be shipped off for the meat trade. How is that right? Cows are grazing animals, aren't they? Surely it would cost more to feed them when they're living inside than grazing off the pastures. I don't know, I'll get Jill to carry out the necessary research for me when we get back."

"Want me to get the ball rolling now?"

"Yes, why not?"

CHAPTER 5

he Head of the college was a lady called Mrs
Crabtree who was on another call when they
arrived. Her secretary asked Sara and Carla to take a seat in
the reception area until she was free. They hadn't been
seated long before the secretary showed them into an office
and introduced them to the Head.

"Do come in. I'm intrigued, how can I help you today?"

"Thank you for seeing us at such short notice. We're DI
Sara Ramsey and DS Carla Jameson. We're hoping you'll be
able to help us with our enquiries."

"Enquiries into what? Have we done something wrong,
here at the college?"

"No, not at all. One of your pupils was involved in an
incident last night, and we're trying to ascertain his move-
ments before... his death."

Mrs Crabtree sat upright. "His death? That is what you
said, wasn't it?"

"That's correct. We've been with the victim's family this
morning, and they informed us that the victim attended a

woodworking class at the college last night. Would you be able to tell us if he turned up for the lesson?"

"I can check the system. Goodness, this is incredibly hard to believe. Can I have the person's name?"

"It's Harry Brown. I believe he's only been coming here a couple of weeks, although he's enrolled on another course at the college as well, one for poetry."

"Okay, let's see what's showing up on the system." She put on her spectacles and hit a few keys. "Ah, yes, here he is. Yes, he attended the class last night."

"I don't suppose it would be possible to have a word with the teacher, would it?"

"No, Mr Swallow isn't here right now. He has a day job and only comes in a few nights a week. I can give you his number, if that will help?"

"Perfect. What about CCTV footage? Will you allow us to view that from last night?"

"Of course. Anything to help the police. May I ask how Mr Brown died?"

"He was murdered. We need to assess how that happened. If you're telling us he came to his lesson last night, then it must have taken place sometime after. It will be interesting to view the footage, see if anything took place in the car park before he left the premises."

"Gosh, I hope not. Of course you can take a look at the footage. I'll give Brad a ring, he's our security expert."

She picked up the phone and made the call. After getting through to Brad, she had a brief chat with him and asked if he could accommodate Sara's request. His response was to invite Sara to join him in his office.

"There you go, all sorted. I'll ask Maisie to take you down there, it's a bit out of the way."

"You're too kind. Thank you for your help."

"My pleasure. I'm sorry we've had to meet in such circumstances."

Maisie showed them through the winding corridors to an office on the lower ground level where Brad met them.

"Thanks, Maisie," Brad said. "Come in, Officers, and take a seat. Let's see what we can find for you. Do you know at what time this person left the college?"

"No, we're short of leads. The only one we have is that he attended a class last night."

"What type of class? I've got the timetables here."

"Great. Woodworking."

"Ah, yes, it was seven until nine. Do you know if he hung around chatting to someone or did he leave right away?"

"Pass. We know nothing."

"Let's try and fill in the blanks for you. I'll forward it to nine and see what we can find."

Sara watched the clock spin at the top of the screen. Brad slowed the disc down when a bunch of people left the college.

"Can you tell me the age of the person?"

"Mid-fifties," Sara replied.

"Right. What about this group here?" Brad zoomed in to what they had in their hands. "If I'm not mistaken, they all seem to be carrying items made of wood."

"I agree. Can you zoom in on their faces?" Sara leaned forward.

"I can. How's this?"

Sara pointed at the screen. "That's him, top left."

"Okay, let's see where he goes then, shall we?"

They watched Brown part from the rest of the group and head out of the car park.

"That's not going to help us, is it?" Brad said. "Wait, no, he's come back again. Maybe he lost his bearings, thought he'd parked elsewhere. It happens a lot, pupils reporting their cars have been stolen only to find them parked in a different area entirely."

"Can you zoom in on the car for us?"

"I can. Here he's putting what looks to be a tray he's made in the boot and getting into the driver's seat. Uh-oh, what's this? Heck!"

Sara saw someone in a hooded sweatshirt approach the car and take a swipe at Harry Brown. "Shit. This isn't good. Any way we can get a better angle on the attack?"

"No, this is the final camera in that section. Jesus, he's taking a real beating. Damn, if only I'd been out there at the time, doing my rounds. I tend to check the grounds every half an hour unless something else crops up."

"And did that happen last night?"

"Yes, one of the women struggled to get into her locker. I had to assist her. I came back to my office to fetch my master key, which I wasn't carrying at the time."

Their focus returned to the screen. After Harry Brown had been given a severe beating, his broken body was then put in the boot of his car by his attacker, and the vehicle left the college car park.

"That's shocking," Brad said. "I've never seen anything like this before and I never want to again. Do you want a copy of the disc?"

"Yes, please. We'll get it down to the lab, see if they can enhance the picture for us to try and identify the assailant." Sara shook her head. The attack had been vicious through-out, and knowing that Brown had suffered from heart prob-lems, she assumed that he had been near to death when he'd been thrown in the boot. "We'll leave you to it for a moment and have a chat outside."

"Yes, that's fine. It shouldn't take me long."

Sara and Carla stood in the hallway, stunned.

"What the bloody hell was that all about?" Carla said.

"The poor bloke didn't have it in him to put up any kind of fight, and yet, realising that, the killer didn't go easy on him. How do we know he wasn't dead by the time they left here?"

Glancing up and down the corridor, Sara heaved out a sigh. "I feel sick to my stomach, seriously. That was unprovoked and vicious from the moment the killer arrived. If Brown wasn't dead by the time they left, he must have been on the brink of it. What we need to do is get on to the station, ask Craig to check through the cameras in this area. Truth be told, I don't think there's a good enough image of the killer on the footage we've seen here for the lab to enhance."

"I'll do it now." Carla withdrew her phone.

Sara's mind remained with the assault she'd just witnessed. She paced the corridor, her steps becoming increasingly agitated the more the images played in her mind. Rarely had she seen such ferociousness during an attack on a victim. She swallowed, shifting the bile burning her throat. Her thoughts lingering with the victim who'd done nothing to provoke the attack from what she'd witnessed. It was as if the killer had been lying in wait for Brown to leave the college, so the intent was there. It was premeditated.

Carla ended her call. "All actioned. Is there anything else we can be doing while we wait?"

"We can plan what we need to do next."

The door of the security guard's office opened, and he exited the room, disc in hand. "Here you go, it's all on there. Sorry I can't be any further help."

"No, there's no need for you to apologise, what you've supplied us with has been brilliant. We might not be able to make out the attacker, but the assault is there for all to see nonetheless."

"I hope you find who you're searching for, and quickly."

115

"So do we. Thanks again, Brad."

He smiled and then showed them back to the reception area.

THE REST of the day was spent going over the leads that had come their way so far. Craig had worked his magic and successfully tracked the car through Hereford on the ANPR cameras. However, the killer had been crafty and kept his head down as he'd passed the equipment, so they were no further forward on that front.

Sara rang the Environmental Health Department and was told that Daniel Fitt was off for a few days, due to personal reasons, and the rest of the team wouldn't be able to assist with their enquiries because he was the designated officer on the case. Sara decided to send a PC round to his house but frustratingly, she had received a call within half an hour, telling her that Fitt wasn't at home.

The only other lead that needed to be checked was the issue involving the farmer and the fact that some of his neighbours had contacted the police about him.

Carla chased up the details. Three neighbours in total had lodged similar complaints about Sanderson blocking the road leading onto the estate with his farm machinery and had verbally abused some of the residents, using threatening behaviour if they dared to confront him about the issues. On each occasion, the police had warned him to address his future conduct, but it hadn't gone any further. That was typical in Sara's opinion. Due to the cuts in the budget, these types of misdemeanours rarely got past the first base.

Sara rubbed her temples and announced, "Okay, let's call it a day. I've had enough, I'm sure you guys have as well. Good work on all we've achieved today. Let's hope we start making headway with the investigation tomorrow."

The team drifted off, leaving Carla and Sara to ensure all the computers and lights were turned off before they left for the evening.

"I'd call that a great day's work, wouldn't you?" Carla said.

"I'm happyish. I'd be even happier if Craig had come up trumps with an ID for the perp, but I suppose it's still early days yet."

"I have a positive feeling about this. The killer seems careless to me. He pounced on Brown in an open place with his intention set in stone, not caring if he was disturbed or not."

"I got that impression as well. Focused on the victim as if he was the only person in the car park that night. But what if there had been someone else nearby? Would he have thought twice about attacking Brown or not?"

"I don't think he would have, but then, I could be talking out of my arse. It wouldn't be the first time."

Sara smiled. "No comment. Come on, let's go home. How are you feeling at the end of your second day?"

"A little tired, but my enthusiasm hasn't dulled in the slightest. So, all good from my perspective. You look exhausted. It's not just the case causing that, though, is it?"

"No, I'm worried about Mark and his mum."

"Hopefully they will have caught it before it's had a chance to spread."

"We should find out tomorrow. It'll be good to get home and be with him tonight."

They made their way down the stairs and out to the cars.

"Have a great evening, Carla."

"Take care, Sara. Call me if you need anything, okay?"

"I'll do that."

The twenty-minute drive home happened on autopilot, with Sara in a daze throughout most of it. It was only inter-rupted by the blast of the horn from a car coming in the opposite direction when she drifted into the other lane at the bottom of the steep hill that led to her home.

"Blimey, that was a close one. I need to pay more attention, especially on that stretch of the road."

When she arrived home, she noticed Mark's car was missing. It was six-fifteen. She couldn't remember him telling her that he had a late surgery or an important operation on his schedule for that day, but then, he'd barely said two words to her since he'd heard the news about his mum.

Misty welcomed her as usual, with an eager purr and a twinkle in her green eyes. Sara swooped down and swept her cat into her arms. They snuggled into each other, and Misty's purring intensified.

"Hello, Munchkin, have you missed me?"

Misty wriggled out of her arms and led Sara into the kitchen where she topped up her water and food bowls. It wasn't until Sara finished taking care of Misty's needs that she spotted the folded note leaning against the kettle. She tore across the room to read it.

GONE TO MY PARENTS'. *I don't know when I'll be back. They need me.*
Mark

THE NOTE WOUNDED HER. It was blunt and to the point, lacking in further detail, and furthermore, omitted any kisses after Mark's name. Why? Misty's meowing broke into her wayward thoughts. She opened the back door to let her out and glanced up at the sky, seeking answers.

"What's gone wrong with my marriage? Or is that me imagining things aren't right between us? I know we're dealing with uncertain times but... Mark has never stopped talking to me like this before. So why now, when he needs me the most because of what's going on with his mother?"

She spent the next five minutes in the same position, looking at the stars that shimmered between the odd cloud, mesmerising her, but they failed to deliver any answers. She was left dealing with a quandary of massive proportions: should she give Mark a call or leave him? Judging by the tone of his note, she was inclined to leave things as they were.

In the end, her weariness took the decision out of her hands. She fixed herself a piece of toast, smothered it in peanut butter and went to bed. Misty ran past her and into the bedroom. Again, her autopilot kicked in. She showered, purposefully avoided getting her hair wet, then slipped under the quilt before she realised what was happening. Once her head hit the pillow, she went out like a light. Two hours later her phone tinkled, announcing that a text had arrived. She put out a hand to collect her phone, almost knocking it on the floor in her daze, and read the message.

WHAT? Are you not at home yet? Did you see my note?

SHIT, damned if I do and damned if I don't. She texted back: *Sorry, yes, I found your note, but I thought I'd leave it up to you to call me. I didn't want to intrude on your family time. XX*

AND THERE WE HAVE IT, it always has to be down to me, doesn't it? Forget it. I'll ring you if I need you, but I wouldn't hold my breath if I were you. M.

. . .

WHAT THE HECK was he talking about? Why the animosity towards her? What had she done? Her nerves jangling, she sat up, fluffed the pillows up behind her and rang him. His phone remained unanswered for several agonising seconds until finally he answered.

"What do you want, Sara?"

"What do you mean? Why are you being like this, Mark? What's going on? Have I done something to upset you? If I have, I wish you'd tell me so that we can sort it out."

"In case you haven't noticed, I have more important things on my mind right now. Mum is really sick and needs all the care and attention I can give her."

"I'm sorry to hear that, I truly am. How is she?"

"Sick. Very sick. They're operating tomorrow."

"Oh, I thought she was having the scan tomorrow."

"They brought it forward a day. Dad rang me, asked me to come right away. They're both struggling, not just Mum."

"Oh, Mark. Why didn't you call me? I could have arranged to take a few days off work and come with you."

"Because you're working an important case. I didn't want to burden you with my family's problems."

"*Your family*? Aren't they my family as well?"

"You've met my parents once before, Sara, you hardly know them. It's better this way. It would have been awkward having you here with us."

His words slapped her hard around the face. "Oh, I see. I didn't know you felt like that, Mark. Is everything all right between us?"

"I don't know, is it? I have to go, Mum needs me."

And that was the end of the conversation. He hung up on her before she had a chance to respond.

She tossed the phone on the bed, seething.

How dare he speak to me like that! It's as though he's blaming me for what's going on with his mother's health.

She threw back the quilt and marched downstairs. There, she opened the fridge and poured herself a large glass of white wine. Aware she was far too wound up to sleep, she sat at the kitchen table for a few minutes then moved into the lounge and switched on the TV. It was still only ten-thirty. She caught the end of the local news bulletin which mentioned both cases she was working on, but thankfully, they hadn't linked them in the media as yet. She knew it would only be a matter of time before they did that.

Her thoughts returned to the state of her marriage. She gulped down a large mouthful of wine and shook her head.

What the hell is going on? Mark has always been the placid sort.

That was true. It had only been the last couple of months since she'd seen a stark change in him. She thought long and hard, trying to remember when the change had happened. But she struggled to come up with the answer. Tired, she pulled the blanket off the back of the sofa and snuggled down under it, her drink forgotten, and promptly fell asleep.

She woke up at ten minutes to six the next morning with Misty jumping all over her legs. "Hello, girl, did you miss me? I'm sorry, I decided to spend the night on the couch." Sara turned off the TV and took her half-filled glass into the kitchen. She prepared some cereal and milk, but her queasy stomach rejected it as soon as she revisited the conversation she'd had with Mark the previous evening.

Sensing her marriage was in jeopardy, she decided it would be for the best not to dwell on it. It was too complex an issue to deal with on her own. Instead, she climbed the stairs and got ready for work. When she came down again, Misty was sitting by her bowl, begging for her breakfast. She filled the dish with dried biscuits and topped up her water, then she opened the back door and let Misty out.

Misty did her business and returned to eat her breakfast.

Sara ensured the back door was locked and left the house. Outside, she bumped into her neighbour, Ted, who was just coming back from his walk with Muffin the poodle.

"Hello, stranger. How are things?" he asked.

"I'm fine. Sorry we've not been over in a while. You know how it is, we both have busy schedules, and by the time we've finished our shifts we're exhausted."

"Hey, don't stress about it. You know where we are if you ever need us."

Sara smiled, grateful he'd accepted her excuse. "How are you both?"

"Mavis has had a touch of flu this week, so I'm doing my bit to make her comfortable."

"Oh, no. Send her my best wishes. Do you need me to fetch you anything back from the shops later? It's no bother, I can stop off at the supermarket for you."

"You're a gem, always thinking of others when you should be taking care of yourself and that wonderful husband of yours. Talking of which, where is he? I haven't seen him around lately."

"He's visiting his parents in Anglesey. His mother has some serious health issues. He wanted to go up there and support them."

"He's amazing. You both are. Oh, well, I don't want to hold you up, I appreciate how hectic your days can be. If you need some company while he's away, drop over. Mavis would love to catch up with you."

"I might just do that. I'm dealing with a double murder case at present, there's no telling when I'm going to get home. I'll see how I go later, if that's all right?"

"Of course it is, no pressure from us. You take care of yourself out there, Sara. We're always thinking about you."

"I will, don't worry. See you later." She continued her journey to her car with tears welling up.

Before Mark had come on the scene, Ted and Mavis had welcomed her onto the exclusive estate and cared for Misty for her when long days had blighted her life. She regarded them as her extended family. Early on in their relationship, the couple had confided in her about the grave loss they'd endured when their twenty-two-year-old daughter had died on a backpacking holiday in Australia. It had rocked their world, but since they'd met Sara, it had softened the blow. That's why she was riddled with guilt now because, since Mark had been around, she had neglected them. She made a mental note to pick up a bottle of wine and a bouquet of flowers for Mavis during the day to make amends.

CHAPTER 6

*T*he news wasn't good when Sara arrived at work. The desk sergeant, Jeff, was on the phone and stared at her, his eyes widening as she stepped towards him.

"What's going on?" she mouthed.

"I'll let her know. Secure the area, and I'm sure the inspector will be with you shortly."

Sara pointed at her chest. "Are you talking about me?"

Jeff ended the call. "Yes, bad news, ma'am. You need to get over to the garage Allan Smith runs. It's on the edge of the city, down by the large estate agent. Damn, I can't think of the name of it now."

"Don't worry, look up the garage and give me the post-code. Why? What's wrong? You mentioned secure the scene. Don't tell me he's dead?"

Jeff nodded. "Afraid so. His colleague found him hanging from the A-frame when he got there first thing."

"Shit. I knew he was angry and emotional yesterday, but I wouldn't have put him down as suicidal, not in the slightest. Is Carla here yet?"

The door closed behind her. "Did someone mention my name?"

"We've got to go. Jeff, will you inform the rest of my team what's going on? Tell them I'll be in touch soon."

"Of course, ma'am."

Sara spun Carla around and gently shoved her towards the door. "I'll fill you in en route."

"Sounds ominous. Don't tell me another murder has been committed?"

"No, it's worse than that."

Carla peered over her shoulder and tutted. "What do you mean? No crime can be worse than murder."

Sara didn't respond until she was sitting in the car. She started the engine and set off. "We're going to Allan Smith's place of work."

Carla faced her and asked, "Why? I don't understand."

"He was found hanging at the premises."

"Shit! How? Not suicide?"

"Looks like it. I didn't think he was the type. Who knows what goes through someone's mind when they lose a loved one, especially a parent?"

"Not only that, don't forget you told him his father was cheating on his mother. Hearing that news might have sent him over the edge."

"True. Damn, why did I have to tell him? I've screwed up big time."

"You haven't. You have no idea the impact divulging that type of information is likely to cause to some people's lives. His mother took the news in her stride, didn't she? Shit, does she know?"

Sara rubbed the back of her neck. "I don't know. I should have asked. Ring Jeff, ask him."

Carla made the call and ended it within a few seconds. "No, Jeff thought that would be down to you."

"Geesh, thanks. There are times when I regret being an inspector. This is one of those times."

Sara arrived at the garage and pulled up alongside the pathologist's van. "You got here quickly, were you already en route? Hang on, you don't usually show up when it's a suspected suicide, do you?"

"Good morning to you, too, ladies. You're going to need to get togged up before you go inside."

"Why are you avoiding my question?"

"I wasn't, sorry, not intentionally anyway. Get suited and booted and you can see for yourself what's going on inside."

Sara glanced at Carla and shrugged. "I guess it's not a suicide after all."

"Now then, did I say that?"

"I think you did by refusing to answer my question."

"You're too sharp for me, DI Sara Ramsey. Come on, get on with it, time is a wasting for all of us, especially you."

"We're going as fast as we can." Sara jumped up and down until the suit fitted close to her crotch.

Carla did the same with less effort. "Why do you always have to make a song and dance out of it?"

Lorraine sniggered.

Sara shot them both a filthy look. "You've got your way of getting dressed and I have mine, never the twain shall meet."

"Whatever," Carla said and flicked her wrist at Sara.

Lorraine finished removing the equipment she needed from the back of the van and then said, "Feel free to lend me a hand, ladies. I'm a tech down today."

"Yeah, we're a team member down at the moment, too, but you don't see us asking you to lend us a hand, do you?"

"Harsh, Inspector Ramsey. I thought you were better than that."

The three of them laughed, collected the equipment and made their way to the garage entrance.

"You might need to prepare yourselves," Lorraine warned.

Sara didn't like the sound of that one iota. She paused, sucked in a couple of steadying breaths and blew them out. "Are you all right about this?" she asked her partner.

Carla shrugged. "I'll soon find out. I know where the exit is if it becomes a problem for me. Don't worry, I won't do a Barry on you."

"Thank fuck for that," Lorraine mumbled and swept past them both, a bag in each of her hands.

Carla pulled a face behind her back, and Sara had to suppress a giggle.

"Let's see what Lorraine is on about." Sara's gaze immediately rose to the ceiling, and she closed her eyes. "Oh shit. I should have guessed."

"Oh shit, indeed," Carla said. She cleared her throat and took a few steps closer to the swinging body of the angry young man she'd met recently.

Lorraine watched them in silence for a moment or two. "Have you seen enough? I think it's time for us to get him down now, don't you?"

"Yes, do it. I'm surprised he's still in situ, if you must know," Sara said.

"I didn't see any reason to get him down, not when it was obvious from the outset that he was dead."

Sara took in the amount of blood pooling beneath Smith's body. "Any idea what happened to him? Without stating the obvious."

"Hard to tell. There are a lot of tools strewn across the floor and in the pit to your right. The killer might have used some of them to torture the victim, but we won't know for sure until the guys have completed their examination. Either that or the victim put up a fight, spilled the tools and tipped over the trolley they were on in an attempt to escape."

Sara scanned some of the tools closest to her feet. "I think your first theory is going to be the winner. There's some blood on a couple of wrenches here."

Lorraine clicked her fingers to gain the attention of the two techs unpacking the equipment beside her. "Will one of you bag those before they get disturbed?"

The younger man dipped his hand into a case and withdrew a couple of evidence bags. Sara took a few steps closer to the victim and studied how his body had been raised. The other end of the tow rope around his neck had been tied off to a sturdy hook attached to the far wall.

"Poor bloke really suffered, just like his dad."

"What a way to go," Carla added.

"All right to lower him now, Lorraine?" one of the techs said. He was standing close to the body with a colleague, a plastic sheet to the side of them.

"Yes, you know the drill. Have you taken all the photos you need to take, Mike?"

"All done."

Sara watched as another tech appeared and took the strain on the rope. The two men standing below the body swung it over to the side and lowered Smith onto the sheet.

"Any missing parts, or is it too early to tell?" Sara asked.

"Two ears were found on the shelf at the rear. His eyes haven't been located yet, and we're still looking for his tongue."

Sara puffed out her cheeks a couple of times. "Jesus, how the fuck am I going to tell his mother?"

"Carefully and respectfully," Lorraine suggested.

"And the colleague who found him is where? I can't see him anywhere."

"He was in shock, so I sent him home. I asked one of the uniformed officers to take his details down."

"I'll check. Did he see anyone hanging around when he got here?"

"Ouch, nice choice of words in the circumstances. No. I did ask."

"It slipped out, sorry. Do you need us for anything else? Only I think we should speak to his mother before she hears about her son's death through the media."

"I agree. We're going to be a while here. Needless to say, I believe we're looking for the same person who killed the other victims, his father included. Therefore..."

Sara held up a hand to prevent Lorraine from finishing her sentence. "We've got a serial killer on the loose."

"Sadly, that's true. A suggestion if I may?"

"Go on," Sara said.

"Far be it for me to tell you your job, but it might be a good idea for you to offer the mother some form of protection, at least until the killer has been found."

"Already thought about it. I'll check with the station to see what properties are available, if any."

"And before you ask, I haven't had a chance to type up the reports as yet. Only because I've had my back against the wall. I had a family who perished in a fire to deal with yesterday."

Sara wrinkled her nose. "Yeah, we don't need to know the details. Whenever you can. I don't suppose you've stumbled across any evidence at either of the scenes?"

"Nope, you're correct, we haven't. What about you, have you found out anything of importance yet?"

"We've got the killer on CCTV footage, attacking the second victim in the college car park where he attended a class the night he was attacked. Also, we're following up leads on a farmer who has been a naughty boy in connection with the second victim."

"A naughty boy, eh? In what way?"

"Harry Brown's family have made several complaints to the Environmental Health about him in the past but nothing recently. The farmer has also been reported to the police for threatening behaviour towards some of their neighbours. It's all going to take time to chase up. We're doing our best, but with a man down, we're going to struggle, especially if we have yet more victims to contend with."

"Very inconvenient. What's wrong with these killers, eh?" Lorraine grinned.

Sara slapped her arm, making her suit rustle. "I can do without your wisecracks as well."

"Where would you be if you didn't have me to brighten your day?"

"I refuse to answer that in case I incriminate myself."

"We should go," Carla reminded Sara.

"You're right, partner, we should. Sorry to run out on you like this, Lorraine, but needs must."

"I won't be shedding any tears over your departure. Do me a favour, if you will?"

Sara inclined her head. "Another one?"

"Sod off! Will you send me a text when you get there, just to let me know his mum is all right?"

"If you want me to." Sara noticed something strange in Lorraine's eyes. "Are you okay?"

"I'm fine. Don't worry about me. I'm just fed up, having to cut open entire families, that's all. You might not think my job gets to me day in, day out, but sometimes that's just not true."

Sara smiled. "Always here if you need a chat, you know that." She had seen a change in Lorraine, one that was hard to put her finger on had been there since Sara and her team had rescued Lorraine from the clutches of a madman several months before.

"I know. You've never let me down yet. Now piss off out of our hair and let us get on with processing the crime scene. I'll get back to you later if anything shows up."

"Please do."

Sara and Carla left the garage and dumped their suits in the black sack just outside the door, by the cordon.

Once they were on the road again, Carla said, "Shit, I feel sorry for Gail and what she's about to go through. No mother should have to deal with the loss of a child so soon after losing her husband."

"Especially if it's because of foul play and obviously by the same killer."

"Yeah, another part that I'm not relishing telling her."

"Ha, as if it would be down to you to tell her anyway. It's muggins here who has the honour of doing all the dirty work."

Carla turned and smiled. "Maybe there are plus sides to you having a higher rank than me after all."

Sara raised her middle finger, and they both laughed. It felt good to lighten the load on her shoulders, if only briefly. She sensed they were in for a traumatic time ahead of them.

GAIL'S SMILE turned into a frown as soon as she saw them standing on her front doorstep. "Oh no, don't tell me something has happened to my son now?"

"Can we come in, Gail?" Sara asked, her insides twisting into knots.

Gail's hands dropped by her sides, and her shoulders slumped in defeat. "I haven't seen him since he left the house yesterday. I thought he'd stayed out all night just to punish me, it wouldn't be the first time. That's why I didn't bother raising the alarm, and now you're here to tell me the worst, aren't you?"

Sara and Carla entered the hallway, and Carla closed the front door.

Sara reached out her arms to Gail. "I'm so sorry. There was nothing we could do to help him."

Gail's legs gave way beneath her. Despite Sara's best efforts, she struggled to prevent the woman from falling. Gail rested her head against the cupboard under the stairs and sobbed.

Carla sprang into action. She squeezed past them and into the kitchen. Sara heard the kettle boiling seconds later. She was in a daze of her own. Numbness had descended and was hard to shift. Carla appeared with a mug of tea for Gail, which she placed on the console table in the hallway, on an envelope, rather than mark the furniture.

"Come on, Gail. Let's get you up and into the lounge, you'll be more comfortable in there."

Carla stood one side of Gail, and Sara moved to the other. Together, they managed to get the older woman to her feet without much effort.

Gail shrugged them off. "I'm okay. I can do this on my own."

They followed her into the lounge. Carla picked up the mug of tea and placed it on the coffee table in front of where Gail was sitting.

"How? How did he die?" Gail asked, her voice frail, trembling with emotion.

"He was found at his workplace this morning. I'd rather not go into details about how he died, but we believe the same person who killed your husband also killed your son."

Gail covered her face with her hands. "No, no, no. Why? How could someone do this to us? Heartless, that's what it is." Her hands dropped, and through the tears, she asked,

"Haven't they punished me enough? Why take my son as well? None of this makes any sense to me. Who could this person be?"

"We're doing our very best to figure that out. I have to tell you that the murderer struck again yesterday, so we're dealing with two investigations, actually three now, at the same time."

"Does that mean my husband's case will be pushed down the list? Forgotten about?"

Sara shook her head. "No, nothing could be further from the truth, I promise you."

"What are you saying then? That the person who killed my husband has taken another life and then come back for my son, is that it?"

"Yes, so it would seem. Do you know where your son went yesterday?"

"You know as well as I do that he marched out of here to see *that woman*. Maybe you should be at the office, grilling her instead of hounding me. I'm sorry, I'm struggling to digest this news. I can't believe Allan has gone now, as well as his father."

"Don't worry, that's going to be our next call. We needed to come and see you first, to break the news. Is there anyone else you can think of who might hold a grudge with your family? Anyone in the past? It needn't necessarily be recent."

"Not at this time. All I can think about is the pair of them, my husband and son, both lying with a sheet over them at the mortuary. I don't think that image is ever going to leave me, nor should it. What have we ever done to deserve this? I really think you need to be grilling *that woman*, yes, she's bound to know. It's too much of a coincidence, isn't it?"

"We'll go and see her, it would be remiss of us not to. Can you think of a reason why she would want to hurt your husband and your son, though?"

"You mean apart from the obvious, of her having an affair with my husband? Who knows what goes through the mind of a person like that when they're desperate to have someone who doesn't belong to them?"

"This is probably a long shot, but do you happen to know a Harry Brown from Withington?"

"What? Harry, yes, of course we... I know Harry. May I ask why?"

"Unfortunately, he's another victim we're dealing with. Can I ask how you know him?"

"Oh my, could this day get any worse? He's one of our dearest friends. We used to be neighbours until a few months ago. We lived out on the Withington estate."

"You lived next door to him and Alice, is that what you're telling me?"

"Yes. We both moved to the estate as the houses were being built around us. Goodness, is Alice okay? I should give her a call."

"Can you put that on hold for now? I really need to get to the bottom of this. Alice and Emily, her daughter, told us they'd had problems with the farmer who lives adjacent to the estate. Tell me, did you have any issues with him when you lived there?"

"Yes, lots of problems. We had to call the police a few times, not that anything was ever done about the bloody man. He's a law unto himself, that one. A vile human being. Selfish to the core, and don't ask me how he treats his animals, it's shocking what I've witnessed him doing to those cows, especially when he thought no one was looking."

"How awful, and I take it you reported the abuse to the correct authorities?"

"Yes, but again, they didn't want to know. That's not quite true, they'd show up because they have to once someone makes a complaint, but the number of times I

peered over the fence during their visits and saw him laughing and joking with them... well, you have to wonder if it's worth all the hassle calling the Environmental Health or sending them an email, if all they're going to do is come down on the farmer's side. We'd had a couple of years of banging our heads against the wall and decided enough was enough. We sold the house, lost money on it, but we didn't care in the end. We were free of that horrible man and the noise and smell from that sodding farm. It was horrendous at times. More often than not, he'd check if you had your washing on the line and purposefully start shovelling the cows' shit from one area to another so that the smell lingered in the air all day. I can't tell you how many times I've had to rewash our clothes over the years. I ended up drying it inside the house just so it remained smelling fresh when I put it away in the wardrobes. It's the little things that turn out to be major things in this life that truly make the difference to your well-being. He's a vindictive bastard, and that's coming from someone who always thinks the best of people."

"We're delving into the complaints now. Once we've gathered all the evidence together, then we intend visiting the farmer."

"And don't forget to pay that man at the Environmental Health a visit, too. He's what I would call a smarmy so-and-so. Says the right things to your face, but as soon as he ends the call, I bet he sits there and sticks two fingers up at the phone. That's the impression I got from dealing with him."

"Yes, we have every intention of speaking with him. Unfortunately, he's off work at the moment with family problems."

Gail plucked a tissue from the box in front of her and dried her eyes. "Is he now? Isn't that a tad convenient? Not that I'm trying to tell you how to do your job, but seriously, you need to dig deep into his background. I'm sure you'll unearth a plethora of trouble."

"We'll be sure to do that. Can we focus on you for now? I would feel much happier if you went and stayed with either a member of your family or a friend, just for the time being, until we've caught the killer."

"No, I don't have anyone else, not really."

"What about if I arrange for you to stay at a secret location for the next few days? Will you agree to that?"

"I'd much rather stay here. I've never really been one for leaving my home and the familiar surroundings of my family. I shouldn't need to be driven from my own home. Isn't that what the police are for, to protect us?"

"It is. However, there's only a certain amount we can do. If I can find a house for you, will you take me up on the offer? I know it will be an inconvenience. Let's put it this way, I'd feel better knowing that you were safe and out of harm's way."

"I'll consider it. At this time, I need to get my head around losing my son, nothing else matters."

"I understand, but we also need to keep you safe at the same time."

"Can't you put a policeman on the door to act as a deterrent?"

"If I have to then, yes, I'll do that. I still think the best option would be for you to stay elsewhere, just as a temporary measure."

Gail shook her head. "If there's an alternative then I'd rather stay here. I'm sorry if that's not what you want to hear, but I've made my decision."

"The choice is yours. I'll call the station, see if they've got a spare officer willing to come out to protect you."

"Thank you, I'd appreciate that."

Sara left the room to make the call, but first she texted

Lorraine to tell her all was well. "Jeff, hi, it's DI Ramsey. I need your help. I'm out at Gail Smith's house; her son and husband have both been murdered over the last couple of days. I'm very concerned for her safety. I've tried to persuade her to move into a safe house if one is available. A member of my team is looking into that for me; however, the lady is insistent that she remains in her own home, in familiar surroundings."

"I can understand her wanting to do that, ma'am, I think I would feel the same way. What do you need from me?"

"Have you got a spare team member who can come over to be with her?"

"Stand guard?"

"Yes, although if the weather is rough, I'm sure she won't mind them coming inside the house. I'd need to run that past her first, but I can't see her objecting to that plan."

"I'll see what I can do for you, ma'am. Can you give me half an hour to check the rotas and what duties I've designated for the day?"

"You do that. We'll be leaving here soon, I hope. I can always contact Gail later, let her know what's been arranged if I need to."

"Leave it with me."

"Thanks, Jeff." Sara ended the call and took a moment to gather her thoughts. Her heart went out to the woman. On the other hand, she felt obligated to keep her safe, knowing the killer was still out there. *Maybe I have something else up my sleeve that I can revisit later, if necessary.* She set that thought aside for now and returned to the lounge.

Carla had changed seats and had her arm draped around Gail's shoulders while the woman sobbed. Carla appeared fretful, out of her comfort zone, and heaved out a sigh that Sara took to be relief.

"Hopefully DI Ramsey will have some news for you,"

Carla said awkwardly. She returned to her seat and picked up the notebook and pen she'd placed on the table in front of her.

Sara smiled. "I have. I've rung the station. The desk sergeant has agreed to place an officer outside your property until further notice. He's in the process of going through the rotas to see who is available and will get back to me in a little while."

"I can't thank you enough. I appreciate this probably isn't the norm in such circumstances. And thank you for taking my feelings into consideration."

"That's what we're here for. Is there anything else we can do for you before we leave?"

"I don't think so. I'm sure I will be fine. The last thing I want to do is be a distraction, prevent you from carrying out your duties in your search for the person responsible for ripping my family apart."

"Don't worry, we can do both at the same time. Having an officer on duty outside will be peace of mind for all of us. I might have told the sergeant that in the event of the weather turning nasty the officer would be welcome to come inside the property. I hope that was okay with you?"

"Absolutely. Thank you for your kindness again, both of you. I don't think I'd be able to get through this ordeal if I had another team working on the investigation."

"We do our best. You've got my number. Any problems, or if anything else comes to mind, give me a call."

"I will. Thank you."

SARA HAD a lot to consider on the drive to the accountants' office. "I think this will be a quick in-and-out job and then we can get back to the station."

"What are you thinking?"

"My thoughts are all over the place. At present, I have two suspects in mind."

"Let me guess, the farmer and the mistress, right?"

"Correct. The only stumbling block I can see is the way the victims were killed. Would a woman be able to overpower the male victims? Don't forget we've already caught a glimpse of the killer on CCTV. Did that look like a woman to you?"

"Nope. I think Brown would have been able to have put up more of a fight if his attacker had been female. All right, I have another notion for you to consider."

"What's that?"

"What if the mistress had an accomplice, a male she's working with?"

Sara chewed over the suggestion for a few moments and then replied, "But if she was in love with Joshua Smith, why would she then kill him?"

"Romances turn sour for all sorts of reasons, especially extra-marital affairs. Don't forget he told her he was putting funds away for their future together and she was contributing to the account, only for him to keep the money. What if she's lied to us and she discovered the truth, that Joshua hadn't been putting the money in the new joint savings account?"

"Plausible, I suppose. Working on gut instinct, I didn't really pick up anything dubious about her when we interviewed her, did you?"

Carla sighed. "That's true. On the other hand, don't you think it's a bit suspicious the son dying? I mean, immediately after he told us he was going to the firm to confront her about the affair?"

"Again, I'm on the fence. Let's see what she has to say about it first."

Sara drew up in Tesco's car park and, together, they

walked up the alley to the accountants' office. "Depending on how this goes, I might shout you lunch at the café we've just discovered."

"Oh, sounds promising, only it's my turn to pay and, well… I'm still a little short."

"We've had this conversation before, good things come in small packages."

Carla tutted. "Ha-bloody-ha, you know damn well what I was talking about."

Sara grinned. "Stop whining. I can afford to shout you a cheap lunch now and again."

"We'll see. You know I don't take kindly to handouts and that I like to pay my way when I can."

"I know. Let's see what happens. We might not even fancy having anything to eat once we've spoken to Maureen."

Another few steps, and Sara pushed open the door to the accountants' office. Maureen immediately glanced their way and seemed panic-stricken.

She came towards them and said, "Hello, is there something wrong?"

"Can we talk to you privately? Unless you want the other staff to hear what we have to say."

"No. Out the back is fine. I won't be long, Paula."

"I need those reports back to me within a couple of hours, Maureen, I made that perfectly clear when I handed them to you earlier."

Maureen groaned. "I know, and they will be. This shouldn't take long."

Sara and Carla did their best to keep up with Maureen, but she was a woman on a mission and had lit up a cigarette in the staffroom by the time they joined her.

"You seem a little anxious, Maureen, may I ask why?"

Maureen motioned for them to take a seat at the table and joined them, bringing the ashtray with her. "Sorry, I know it's considered rude to smoke in public these days, are you okay with it?"

Sara shrugged. "Don't mind us. What's going on?"

"Nothing. I'm presuming you've come to see me because of the altercation I had with Allan yesterday."

"How did that pan out?"

"He said some vile things to me, in front of the other staff and a client who was just about to leave after having a meeting with Ralph. I couldn't stand it any more. Allan wouldn't believe me when I told him how much I loved his father. He proceeded to call me every name going under the sun. I couldn't take it... a moment longer."

Sara inclined her head. "What did you do?"

"I let loose and struck him. My own frustration and emotions overwhelmed me, and I couldn't hold back a second longer. I kept lashing out at him. I found myself hating him for spending so much time with his father over the years, time that I should have had with him and missed out on."

"And what happened then? Did he retaliate?"

"That was the weirdest part, no, he took every hit I had in me and then left. He shrugged, turned and walked out of the door."

"Where did he go?"

"How should I know? I was relieved to see him leave. Paula hugged me, told me how brave I was to confront him. I didn't feel brave. I felt terrible. I shouldn't have done it, lashed out like that. He didn't deserve it, but then, I didn't deserve the way he spoke to me either. Can I ask why you've come to see me?"

Sara inhaled a breath, and her gaze latched on to Maureen's. "Because this morning, we were called to Allan's place of work where his body was found. He'd been murdered."

"What? This can't be true. How? After his father died a few days ago? I don't understand how this can happen."

"Believe me, neither do I."

"Are you sure he was murdered? Umm… the mood he was in, he appeared to be a bit unstable. What if he took his own life?"

"We're sure. We believe he died at the hands of the same person who killed his father."

Maureen frowned and puffed on her cigarette. "Did someone see the killer?"

"No, we haven't found any witnesses as yet."

"Then how do you know?"

"Because he died from the same injuries as Joshua."

"Jesus. This is unbelievable. His poor mother. Oh God, is she all right?"

"Yes, we've got her under police protection until we can find the killer. I have to ask, where were you last night?"

"I was at home. I managed to talk my husband round, because I didn't have anywhere else to go. Anyway, I slept in the spare room, drowning my sorrows. Allan wiped the floor with me during his unexpected verbal attack. I felt worthless and went straight to bed when I got home with a bottle of vodka and a packet of crisps. I woke up this morning with a thumping headache. To tell you the truth, it's only just worn off."

"Can anyone corroborate your alibi?"

"Yes, my husband. You can't believe that I could be guilty of killing him? *Are you insane*? Not two minutes ago, you told me that he was killed by the same person who had robbed us of his father, and now you're sitting there insinuating that *I* killed him. Why on earth would I do that?"

"Maybe because of the way he spoke to you yesterday."

Maureen slammed her clenched fist on the table. The ashtray jumped into the air and came down on its edge then rolled onto the floor. "Shit, now look what you've done. I had nothing to do with his death. I'm appalled that you should try to pin his murder on me, too."

"It's a lead we needed to follow up on, knowing how angry he was when he came to see you yesterday."

"I could never hurt Allan, let alone kill him, the son of the man I loved. Am I in trouble here?"

Sara sighed and shook her head. "No, I believe you're innocent. We needed to find out what happened after he left here."

"I can't tell you that. Thank God you believe me. How is Gail holding up? I know I don't have a right to ask."

"She seems okay. I'm going to keep a close eye on her over the weekend."

"Good. I'm so sorry about the way things have turned out. It's true what they say, you can't help who you fall in love with."

"No, but most people find restraint is the answer. We'll go now. Thanks for speaking with us."

Sara's harsh words appeared to hit home because Maureen refused to stand and started crying once more.

"We'll see ourselves out," Sara added.

She and Carla left the room.

"Are you all right?" Carla asked once they had left the premises.

"I thought I was, until she asked how Gail was. You know me, I struggle with any form of hypocrisy. If Gail's welfare was a consideration to her, then why would she start an affair with the woman's husband in the first place?"

"Like she said, you can't help who you fall in love with."

"Yeah, and that's a load of bollocks as well. Of course you bloody well can, especially if that person is in a happy relationship with someone else and has a family."

"It's not always the case. You and I know what's right and

wrong in that respect, but not everyone does, not when Cupid's arrow strikes."

Sara stopped walking and stared at Carla. "Are you for real?" she said and laughed so hard that tears ran down her face in no time at all.

"It wasn't that funny. Hey, we're going the wrong way. I thought we were going to stop off at the café for lunch."

"Funny that, I've lost my appetite all of a sudden. We'll grab something from Tesco instead. I can eat it later at my desk, if I get hungry. I need to pick up a pressie for my neighbours if I have the time."

THEY DECIDED to stop off for a selection of sandwiches and shared them around with the others when they returned to the station. Carla made everyone a coffee, and they sat around in a circle, discussing the investigation and the different leads the rest of the team had been following up on while they'd been out.

"Obvious question for you, Craig, have you found anything further, after trawling through the CCTV footage?"

"Not yet, but I sense I'm getting close, boss."

"I know these things take time. Do your best to get an answer for me by the end of the day, if you would?"

"I'll try." He held his thumb and forefinger half an inch apart and added, "I'm this close, I can feel it in my water."

Sara chuckled. "If you say so. Okay, here's what we've learnt today so far. We now know there's a link between all of the victims. They used to be close neighbours and friends before the Smiths moved away from Withington. We're hearing more and more about the problems they've had to contend with over the years from the farm adjacent to the estate where the Smiths used to live and where the Browns still live. We need to chase up any complaints we've received and go through them. I have a feeling that we're going to need as much ammunition we can find against this chap before we tackle him."

"I can chase that up for you," Jill said.

"Thanks. I also rang the EH, and they told me that Daniel Fitt, the officer who has dealt with the complaints from the families in the past, is out of the office for the next few days, dealing with family issues," Sara said. "Saying that, a constable has visited the house a couple of times but hasn't been able to find Fitt in yet."

"Yeah, that's a likely story. Maybe he's in cahoots with the farmer and has been told to keep out of the way," Carla suggested.

"Possibly. We can't rule anything out at this stage. Let's carry out the usual background checks on him all the same, see what shows up." Sara's mobile rang, and she answered it. "Hi, Jeff. What's up?"

"I said I would let you know what was happening. Sorry it's taken so long to sort out. We're a few bodies light at present. I've sent a constable over to Gail Smith's house and I'm just making arrangements for a couple of men to be at the property twenty-four-seven, until you tell me they are no longer needed."

"That's great, Jeff. I really appreciate it. It'll put my mind at ease as well, for the foreseeable anyway."

"You're welcome, glad I could oblige."

Sara ended the call and turned to Christine to ask, "Any news on a safe house?"

"I just breathed out a sigh of relief, overhearing your conversation with Jeff, because I've been told there are no safe houses available in the area."

"That's fine. She was reluctant to leave her familiar surroundings, so having someone on duty outside over the weekend will be a far more appropriate option all round. I'll keep an eye on her now and again myself because my husband will be away over the weekend and I'll only be at home twiddling my thumbs, so I might as well make myself useful. Anything else we've missed?" Sara opened up her email account on her phone and spotted one from Lorraine. "Ah, looks like the PMs are in. I'll read through the reports in my office if there's nothing else?"

"Want me to put a surveillance on the farmer, or is it too soon for that?" Carla asked.

"I don't think we've got any manpower left to do that, Carla. So, we'll leave it for now. Let me read the reports, and I'll get back to you."

She took the remains of her sandwich and what was left of her coffee and relocated to her office, closing the door behind her. Before she opened the email from Lorraine, something in her gut was telling her to give Mark a call. Settled behind her desk and with her stomach tied in knots, she rang him. It was several seconds before he answered.

"Hello."

"Hi, Mark. It's me."

"I'm aware of that. What do you want, Sara?"

Shocked by his tone, she stuttered, "I... umm... I was checking in on you... to see how your mother is... and how you're holding up."

"She's having the operation now. We won't know the results until later and I'm looking after my father who has aged ten years since I got here. Was there anything else?"

"Oh, I see. No. I'll leave you to it then. Send your parents my love."

"If you insist."

Mark ended the conversation before she had the chance to tell him how much she loved him. Tears pricked her tired eyes, but she refused to let the situation get to her. She couldn't afford to get emotional at work, not while running a triple murder investigation. Her professionalism took over, and she opened the email and printed off the reports. Then she leisurely studied them, blocking out any thoughts she might have to do with the state of her marriage.

Reading the reports helped to put life back into perspective for her. There were folks out there, members of the general public, who she had pledged to serve all those years ago as a cadet in training college, who needed her help. Three murders all linked. Three innocent people all killed. Why? Sara struggled to get her head around the farmer killing these people off just because he'd fallen out with them. *That doesn't really happen, does it?* She finished reading through the reports and then joined the rest of the team once more.

"Everything is as expected in the PM reports. No evidence found at any of the scenes, which is a major setback for us. If the farmer is the killer, he's being damned careful about how he kills his victims, which kind of surprises me. Don't ask me why. But I would expect to find something at the scenes, like mud or cow shit perhaps, but once again nothing has shown up."

"You sound like you're ruling him out," Carla said.

"I'm not sure about that just yet. Like I've already said, I think we're going to need to keep an open mind about this, for now."

"Okay, fair enough. We've searched through the complaints from the neighbours. Our guys have had to intervene a few times to warn the farmer about his aggressive behaviour towards the neighbours, however, that was mostly down to hearsay from the residents."

Sara tilted her head. "I don't understand. What are you getting at, Carla?"

"Every time our guys showed up, the farmer has always

been very co-operative and it's been the residents who have been kicking off. Their tone angry."

"Like mob mentality, is that what you're implying?"

"Sounds like it. So, when our guys show up, the farmer puts on a front and stands there acting like the nice guy while the residents throw their dummies out of their prams."

Sara thought over the scenario and nodded. "He's playing our guys."

"So it would seem. I'm going to do some extra digging into his background, see if there are any red flags there."

"And what about Daniel Fitt? Anything showing up on him?"

"We've got his address, that's about it. No police record as such. He's had a few parking tickets to his name, that's all so far."

"Check if anything is showing up via the media, if you would?" Sara moved around the room. "You know what I'm going to ask, Craig?"

"I know, boss. I swear, I'm doing my best. I've never let you down in the past. I'd say we're dealing with a very devious person who knows how to dodge being detected by the cameras."

"Worth consideration. What about the perpetrator's car? He or she, must have got to the college somehow. Maybe they left their vehicle in the car park and… wait a minute, if the killer drove Brown out to Lower Lyde, how the dickens did they get back from there? Are we looking at an accomplice helping them? We have to be, right?"

"You might be on to something. Maybe the other person dropped the killer off at the college and then followed Brown's car out to the crime scene, hung around while the deed was done, and then picked up the killer and dropped them back into Hereford. I'll start searching for the other car on the cameras. I can't say I've noticed anything so far, but then, I haven't really been looking out for any other vehicles."

Sara patted him on the shoulder. "Do your best. Maybe the accomplice held back, didn't travel too close behind, something else you need to take into consideration, Craig."

"I'm going to be a while, if that's the case. Shame Barry isn't around to help me out."

"Marissa, if you haven't got much on your plate, can you give Craig a hand for an hour or two?"

Marissa smiled and walked towards them. "Ready and willing. What do you want me to do, Craig?"

"I'll leave you to it," Sara said and crossed the room to the drinks station to get a refill.

Carla joined her. "Are you okay? You seem a bit down."

"I'm fine. I suppose my frustration is notching up a touch and getting the better of me."

"Don't let it do that. We're doing our utmost with the evidence we have to hand. I can't believe there was nothing found at any of the scenes."

"Neither can I. I think that's what is frustrating me the most."

"Are you sure there's nothing else going on in that head of yours?"

Sara smiled and heaved out a breath. "You know me so well. I just rang Mark. He was really abrupt with me, and he appears to be punishing me at every opportunity that comes his way."

Carla rubbed her arm and then proceeded to make them a coffee. "My advice would be not to read too much into it. He's probably feeling out of his depth dealing with his mother's diagnosis and her forthcoming operation. Hang on, isn't that happening today?"

"Yes, at this moment."

"There you go then. He's probably feeling overwhelmed

and anxious with his mother in the operating theatre. Try and cut him some slack, Sara."

"You're right. I know I'm being an idiot… he's just never spoken to me this way before in all the years I've known him, which is a fair few now. I didn't tell you, I offered to take a couple of days off to go to Anglesey with him, but he said he didn't need me, *his family didn't need me.* That's not what a wife wants to hear from the husband she's head over heels in love with."

"Ouch, no wonder you're feeling like shit about this. I think I'd feel the same if I were in your shoes. You know he loves you, Sara. What you're going to need to do is set this aside for now. I'm not trying to make excuses for Mark, but you have to imagine how difficult this is for him to handle."

"No worse than when I lost my mother. I didn't push him away."

Carla didn't have an answer to that one, so she simply shrugged. Eventually, to break the silence that had descended, she said, "Men are different to women. Give him time, he'll come good in the end."

"I hope so. I dread to think what the alternative will be if he doesn't."

Carla gasped. "Pack it in. You two would never get divorced. I'm telling you now, that man thinks the bloody world of you. When he comes home, why don't you take some time off, perhaps go away together?"

"Because he'll have a backlog to deal with at the practice, that's why."

"Ah, yes. I never thought about that."

"I'm done thinking about it, for now. I need to get my mind back on the investigation. I've been mulling it over, why don't we take a ride out to Daniel Fitt's house, see what he has to say about all of this, if we can catch him in?"

"Are you sure that's the way to go? What if he's more involved in this than we think at this stage?"

"Maybe you're right."

The phone on Jill's desk rang. Sara's ears pricked up when she heard her name mentioned, and she marched towards Jill to see what the problem was.

"Just a moment, I'll pass you over to DI Ramsey now." Jill covered the mouthpiece with her hand. "It's Emily Brown, she's frantic. Her mother has gone missing."

"Shit, no way. I'll speak to her." Sara perched on the desk behind her and answered the call. "Emily, this is Sara Ramsey. What's going on?"

"It's Mum. She put the rubbish out the front, and when I realised she hadn't come back in, I went out to look for her, but she was nowhere to be seen."

"She's gone? Is her car still there? Could she have popped to the shops and not told you?"

"No, she doesn't drive. She's gone, and I don't know where to start looking for her. Please, you've got to help me, you have to."

"Okay, hang tight. I'm on my way." Sara passed the phone back to Jill and ran into her office to fetch her jacket.

Carla was pulling hers on when she returned.

"Come on, Carla, let's go."

CHAPTER 7

*E*mily was in a state of frenzy when Sara and Carla drew up outside the house.

"Okay, calm down. We need to go inside, Emily," Sara said. She guided the young woman through the front door to the kitchen at the rear. "Have you asked the neighbours if they've seen her? Could she have nipped round there for a cup of coffee?"

"No. She would have told me if she had any intention of going anywhere. She's gone, I'm telling you. There's no point in you being here if you're not going to help me search for her."

"Okay. You stay here, and we'll check with the neighbours, see if anyone saw her outside."

Emily sat on the sofa by the window, her head in her hands, and Sara and Carla ran through the house and outside once more.

"You go left, and I'll take the houses on the right," Sara said. "Make it brief, just ask if they've seen Alice within the last hour or so. If they haven't, move on to the next one. Don't get into a conversation with anyone."

"I won't."

They went their separate ways. Sara's heart pounded as she stopped at the first neighbour's house. A woman in her sixties opened the door.

Sara flashed her ID. "Sorry to trouble you. Have you seen Alice in the last hour or so?"

"Alice? From next door? No, I can't say I have. I've been doing the housework all morning. Why? What's happened? Is anything wrong? Is she okay?"

"I'm sorry. I need to go, see if the other neighbours have seen her. Thanks for your help."

She left the woman standing there, her mouth gaping open, and rang the bell to the neighbour next door, and the one after that, and still received the same answer: no one had seen hide nor hair of Alice. Sara's fear escalated to another level; she sensed something serious had happened to Emily's mother. She returned to the Browns' house and waited on the path for Carla to join her.

"Nothing at all. What about you?" Carla asked.

"Zilch. The woman couldn't have just vanished into thin air. I'm going to have a peek over the fence." Sara snuck up to the rear of the property and peered into the farmer's yard.

A tractor was moving from one end of the yard to the other. The farmer was driving it.

Shit, does that mean we've got this all wrong? If he's on site, then maybe he's holding her there. Without any proof, I can't go over there and accuse him of anything, or can I? Shit, shit, shit!

She returned to the front of the house. "He's there. I can't see her, but I didn't really expect to."

"Where do we go from here?"

"I'm going to call for backup and go over there and have a word with him. I'll get extra bodies out here to search the estate thoroughly, just in case Alice is confused and has wandered off somewhere."

"I agree. Bloody hell, even I'm worried about her now."

"I think we should be, after what's happened to the other victims this week. People don't just disappear, do they?"

Sara rang the station and requested the backup, asked the desk sergeant to send his officers to the house and she would instruct them from there. Then she and Carla headed back inside to check how Emily was holding up.

"Hi, none of the neighbours have seen her. I've put in a call for more uniformed officers to attend; they should be here shortly. Does your mum have a phone with her?"

Emily sniffled and pointed to a mobile sitting on the worktop. "No, that's the first thing I did, tried to ring her. Frightened the shit out of me when it started to ring behind me. I hadn't even noticed it sitting on the side before I rang it. I'm worried about her. She never wanders off like this. I'm struggling to come to terms with it, especially after what happened to my father. How can she go missing like this? It's not possible. She's got all her faculties about her; this isn't making any sense to me."

"Try not to think of the worst. She's grieving. All common sense can go out of the window for some people at a time like this."

"No, I dispute that. Mum has been fine since Dad died. In fact, she's been holding it together better than I have. I know when something doesn't feel right."

"Okay, try and remain calm. Getting yourself worked up into a state isn't going to help the situation. As soon as backup arrives, we'll start looking for her in earnest, I promise."

"Why do you have to wait? She needs us. Someone has taken her; they're going to kill her just like they killed my father." Emily sniffled again. "Oh God, please, please don't allow this to happen. What will I do if Mum is taken from me as well? I can't—no, I won't—be able to go on, not without her in my life. My parents meant absolutely everything to me... I can't imagine life without them."

Sara grasped Emily's hands and squeezed them, tears threatening to flow. "Please don't say that. Give us a chance to find her. We won't be able to start the search until backup arrives. It's my job to issue the officers with their orders."

Emily gulped and nodded then collapsed onto the sofa again and placed her head in her hands. "I feel so damn helpless. Maybe I should be out there looking for her myself, I know the estate far better than you."

"I would advise against you doing that. You're needed here, in case she comes back. She might be out there, lost and bewildered for all we know."

"You're wrong. Why won't you believe me? I know my mother inside and out. She would never go off, not without telling me where she was going first."

"Okay, I do believe you."

A knock sounded on the front door. Emily made an attempt to stand, but Sara raised her hand.

"DS Jameson will answer it."

Carla raced through the house and opened the front door to find two uniformed officers, one female and the other male. "Come in."

Sara appeared at the end of the hallway. "Yes, come in. It's Jason and Fiona, isn't it?"

"That's right, ma'am," Jason replied. "The sergeant told us to come straight away. How can we help?"

Sara smiled. "Are there more officers on the way?"

"Yes, another patrol car is around five minutes behind us."

"Okay. The lady of the house has been reported missing." Sara walked towards the officers and lowered her voice. "The woman's husband was murdered earlier this week, which is why I requested backup ASAP. I need you to conduct a thor-

ough search of the area. Carla and I have asked the immediate neighbours, but no one has seen her."

"How long has she been missing?" Fiona asked.

"Between one and a half and two hours. She put the bins
out and just disappeared."

"Is she confused?" Jason asked.

"Not according to the daughter." Sara peered over her
shoulder and leaned in to whisper, "It's not looking good.
We've had three murders in the last three days. We've just
found out they're all connected and the victims were all
killed by the same perpetrator. Two of them were father and
son, killed at different times. That's the urgency here. Alice's
husband was murdered a few days ago, and we can't rule out
the killer coming back to kill her, judging by his past record."

"Holy crap. Okay, ma'am, we'll get out there and start
searching. It might be worth calling in the K9 team to assist
us," Fiona said.

"Good shout. Can you organise that for me?"

"Leave it with me. We'll make a start and get back to you
if we find out anything about the woman. Alice what,
ma'am?"

"It's Alice Brown. Her daughter is Emily, just in case you
return and we're not here. As soon as the other patrol car
arrives, we're going next door to the farm with the intention
of having a nose around."

"May I ask why?" Jason asked. He shuffled his feet. "Sorry,
am I being too inquisitive for my own good?"

"Not at all. There's a suspicion that he might be involved,
although we're having to tread carefully with that information for now, as we haven't found any evidence to back up
our claims. It's a tough call, but I'm determined to help Emily
find her mother, no matter what it takes."

"We get that, ma'am."

Sara smiled and nodded. "Do your best for them both."

The officers left the house.

Carla turned to face her and said, "I can see this getting messy once we go next door."

"Hopefully it won't come to that. Come on, team, where are you?"

"Be patient, they're on their way."

The door to the kitchen opened, and Emily stood there, her expression full of confusion. "Who was at the door? I was hoping you would come back and tell me, not leave me all alone in there, thinking the worst."

"Sorry, we were just on our way back to you. It was one of the backup teams. I've issued them with instructions to search every nook and cranny on the estate for your mother."

"You really think she'll still be around here? I don't. I believe the search should be widened, but I get the impression that you still aren't taking me seriously."

"I can assure you, I am. You're going to have to trust us. I have every intention of issuing a countywide alert for your mother as well. If you have a recent photo of her, can you send it to my phone?"

"Oh yes, just a moment." Emily raced back into the kitchen and returned scrolling through her phone. "I have your number saved, I'm sending it now."

Sara removed her phone from her pocket and opened the text message. "That's an excellent one. Leave it with me, I'll pass it on to the desk sergeant and he can distribute it to his teams out on the streets."

"Thank you. I hope she's found soon. The longer she's missing, the more stressed I'm going to get."

"Why don't I make you a drink while I wait for our colleagues to arrive?"

"I can do it. Would you like one, too?"

"Not for us, thank you. We'll be going soon."

Emily went back into the kitchen, and Sara left the house to make the call to the station.

"Jeff, it's me, pest again. I'm going to send you a photo of Alice Brown, the lady who has gone missing. Can you do the necessary and distribute it for me?" She forwarded the photo to him.

"I've got it, ma'am. Leave it with me. Have the teams arrived yet?"

"Jason and Fiona have already reported to me. We're still waiting for the other team to get here. Can you do me a favour and ask how long they're going to be? I'm eager to get on, can't abide standing around twiddling my thumbs."

"Hold the line and I'll check."

While she waited, Sara's gaze drifted up and down the road.

"They're two minutes away from you now, ma'am."

"Thanks, Jeff. No doubt I'll speak to you again soon."

"Feel free, if you think I can help."

Sara ended the call and then snuck up to the fence again to have a quick nosey into the farmer's yard as everything appeared to be quiet now the tractor had stopped going up and down. The yard was empty, raising Sara's suspicions.

Carla drew her attention a few seconds later. "Psst... the team are here."

Sara nodded and rejoined her partner at the front of the house. "Can you tell Emily that we'll nip back later to see her and to lock the doors until we return, only open it again if she sees a police officer at the door?"

Carla nodded and entered the house. Sara made her way over to the patrol car. The two officers, two fit young males, exited their vehicle and came towards her.

"Hey, thanks for coming out. Sorry to have to get the sergeant to chase you up. I'm eager to see what's going on next door at the farm. What are your names?"

"Steve and Lee, ma'am. Are we still on the hunt for the missing woman?"

"Yes, that's right. There's a distinct possibility the farmer might be involved, except we're struggling to find the proof we need to take things further."

Carla came out of the house and closed the door behind her.

"Are we ready to rock and roll?" Sara asked.

"I'm ready," Carla said.

"We're both good to go, too, ma'am," Steve replied. "Shall we follow you round there?"

Sara was unsure whether to approach the farm on foot or by car. After a moment's deliberation, she said, "Yes, we'll take both cars. Leave the talking to me. I need you to keep your ears and eyes open while we're on the property."

"We'll follow your lead."

They all got back into their respective vehicles, and Sara drove off the estate and into the farmyard. The four of them exited the cars. The farmer came out of the barn on the far side and slid the large door shut behind him.

"Hello, can I help?"

Although he smiled, Sara noticed it never reached his eyes. He stared at her intensely, the way he had earlier, as she stepped forward to speak with him.

"Hi, we're conducting enquiries into a missing person. We're searching the area. There's a possibility that the woman might be dazed and confused."

He raised an eyebrow and folded his arms. "Oh, right, and you're here to ask me if I've seen her, is that right?"

"Yes, also, we wondered if you wouldn't mind us having a look around the property, just in case she's wandered into one of your barns by mistake."

"Okay, umm… don't you need a warrant for that type of

thing? This is private property. I'm sure, had I seen her, I would have sent her on her way."

"If you're telling me I need a warrant then I'll happily apply for one. I thought we wouldn't have to go down that route. But if you have something to hide then we'll get one sorted right away."

The farmer sighed. "I didn't say I had anything to hide. What I'm saying is, we're trying to run a business here and have heavy machinery moving around the yard area non-stop throughout the day. If she had come onto the property either I or my son would have seen her and escorted her from the area, for her own safety, of course."

"That's good to hear. So, you wouldn't mind us having a quick nose around then? Just in these buildings here, close to the yard."

He stared at her, his face expressionless. Sara held his gaze. Numerous men had tried to unnerve her over the years and failed.

He threw an arm up in the air. "Do what you like, your lot usually do anyway, don't you?"

"No, not in the slightest. Thank you for giving us your permission."

He took a step back and leaned against the wall. He was joined by another man shortly after. They had similar features; therefore, Sara presumed the newcomer was his son.

"Okay, Carla and I will take this side of the yard and, Steve, you and Lee start on that side. We'll meet in the middle." She lowered her voice and whispered, "Remember, eyes and ears open at all times. Search high and low. I don't think he's going to allow us to stick around here for long, so spread out as much as you can to cover the area."

"Yes, ma'am," the two officers replied.

Sara and Carla set off towards the two barns on the right,

one of which was open at the front, just an iron gate holding back the dozens of young cows inside it. Sara glanced back at the farmer.

"Feel free to get in there and have a root around, they're friendly enough. Watch out for the cow pats everywhere, though," Sanderson shouted and then laughed.

His son joined in.

"He's got no intention of making this easy for us," Carla mumbled.

"Nope, just keep smiling. I'm going to ease around the side of the building, see if there are any gaps in the structure that will allow me to see inside. I don't relish getting up close and personal with the cattle, do you? The stench is vile."

"Yep, we were warned about the smell. What the heck were the planners thinking, allowing a new estate to be built this close to a working farm?"

"Don't come down on his side. It seems to me that he's doing everything he can to make life difficult for the residents. Whether that makes him a suspect or not is a different story entirely."

They eased their way down the side of the building, gagging a few times because of the stench coming from the cows' urine overflowing from the gulley running the length of the barn.

"Enjoying yourselves, are you?" Sanderson appeared at the top of the track. "Maybe you should have changed into your wellies or slipped on some of those plastic boots before you decided to search around here. Not the brightest idea you're going to have today, is it?" He laughed and left the area before Sara could come up with a quick retort.

"Bastard. Let's hope he'll be laughing on the other side of his face soon."

"Don't let him get to you. He's right about covering our shoes, though. These boots cost me fifty quid in the sale at the end of the summer. They're going to have to go in the bin now."

"Maybe he'll allow us to hose ourselves down before we leave."

Carla stared at her. "Think on. He's a wind-up merchant, you can tell that by just looking at that smug face of his. He's enjoying every minute of our discomfort."

"I think you're right. He's an arsehole. All we need is one piece of evidence to come our way and it'll be a privilege to throw the book at him. That poor woman didn't just wander off, I'm certain of that now. So, we've got to keep searching, because if we don't, I dread to think what's going to happen to her, *if* he has kidnapped her and he's keeping her somewhere on his land."

"You reckon he's likely to keep her close to the road? Do we know how many acres he's got?"

"What are you suggesting? That he kidnapped her and is keeping her elsewhere? Like at the rear of the property?"

"I believe it's more likely than him keeping her a stone's throw from her house, where all the neighbours know her. Why else would he be standing there watching us, laughing at us?"

Sara nodded. "You're right. I've handled this the wrong way, I admit that now. Let's have a cursory glance around, just in case."

"We might as well, now we've come this far and ruined our shoes in the process."

They continued to walk the length of the barn which must have been around sixty to eighty feet long. The cows' mooing was intense and deafening at times, but they carried on regardless. At the end was a grass bank.

"Let's wipe our feet on that, it'll take some of the excess off, at least."

"In your dreams." Carla stared down at her footwear,

unamused. "Is it worth it? We've got another barn to check on this side yet."

"Granted. Okay, let's get that done and worry about the consequences afterwards."

The outside of the second barn was in the same state, which only added to their foul mood.

"Remind me to query the next time you have something like this on your mind. I need to buy a pair of wellies and keep them in the back of your car, just in case."

"Might not be a bad idea. We do live in a farming community, in case you hadn't noticed."

"Yeah, but how often are we forced to sink this low? Not often. I don't think it's ever happened before, has it?"

"Stop whingeing. The quicker we get on with the job in hand, the sooner we can get out of here."

With the second barn checked, they met up with Steve and Lee in the middle of the farmyard once more.

"Anything?" Sara asked.

Steve shook his head, disappointed. "Nothing that we could see, ma'am."

"Same for us. Okay, let's try and clean up our shoes before we get back in the cars."

Sanderson and his son left their positions outside the front of the farmhouse and walked across the yard to join them.

"Everything check out to your liking, did it?" Sanderson asked.

"Absolutely, but then, you knew it would, didn't you?" Sara replied.

He grinned and folded his arms. "I said as much when you arrived. You should learn to trust people, Inspector. It could end up saving you some footwear."

"Talking of which, do you have a hosepipe we can use, please?"

"Ah, here's the thing, it broke yesterday. The lad here needs to nip to B and Q to get a new part to fix it. He's good with his hands."

Sara doubted if what he was telling her was the truth but smiled, even though what she really wanted to do was whack him around the face. "No bother, we can sort it out back on the estate. If you can keep an eye open for this lady, we'd appreciate it. I'll give you my card, just in case." She handed him a card and showed him Alice's picture at the same time to gauge his reaction.

"I know her. Her house backs onto the farm, doesn't it? I've seen her nosing over the fence several times over the years. Shame she's gone missing. Hasn't she recently lost her husband?"

"You seem to be well informed, Mr Sanderson."

"Oh, yes. We like to do our bit for the community, keep our ears to the ground. Help out when we can, like today. That's us, open and obliging, especially where the police are concerned."

Sara kept a smile pinned in place despite seething inside. He was intentionally setting out to rub her up the wrong way.

You fucker. By being over-friendly towards us, all you've done is make me suspect you even more. If you're guilty of kidnapping and hurting Alice Brown, I'm going to string you up myself at the earliest opportunity, mate.

"You're right, you've been super helpful. We can't thank you enough for cooperating with us when you didn't have to."

"You're welcome. Is there anything else you need from us today? If not, we have a full day ahead of us and need to start clearing the shit out of the barns now."

"No, that's all. You carry on, and we'll get out of your hair."

He turned away and mumbled something indecipherable.

"Sorry, I didn't quite catch that. Care to repeat it, sir?" Sara challenged, her pulse racing.

"I said, the weather is going to turn on us soon, so we'd better get on."

"Ah, yes. The forecast is dreary for later on. Thanks again."

Sara rolled her eyes at her colleagues and waited until the farmer was out of earshot before she spoke again. "Cantankerous shithead. He thinks he's got one over on us. I've got news for him. Right, let's get back to the estate, see if someone will let us use one of their hoses, and afterwards, we'll have a conflab about what to do next."

The tractor started up as the four of them marched towards the exit of the farmyard.

"'Ere, ain't you forgetting your cars?" Sanderson shouted from high up in his cab.

"We'll be back in a few minutes."

"They're in the way, I want them shifted. Now."

"Fucking moron," Sara muttered, her smile set firmly in place again. "We'd better keep on his good side." She glanced down at Steve's and Lee's shoes. "Yours don't seem too bad. Have you got any bags in your boot that you can slip over your shoes until we find an available hose?"

"Yes, as it happens, I've got a roll of food bags I always keep with me. I use them as poo bags for when I take the dog out. Yeah, don't ask. I think they'll be up to the task in hand," Lee said.

They all laughed. He went on ahead and tore off two bags for each of them. Sara took a sneaky look at the farmer to see his reaction. He was in the cab of the tractor, laughing with his son.

Sara didn't bother looking in the farmer's direction again, grateful to Lee for coming to their rescue. She sat in the driver's seat and started the car. "We'd better find a water supply soon, otherwise this stuff is going to stink the car out."

Carla gagged. "You're not kidding."

Sara drove back onto the estate and stopped outside the Browns' house. Emily was standing at the front window, watching out for them.

She flew to the door and asked, "Any news yet?" She stared at their feet and gasped. "What the...? What's going on?"

"Umm... I hate to ask this, but is there any chance we can use your hosepipe? The farmer's one was conveniently out of action."

Emily laughed. "I can't believe he would do that to you. Mind you, I'm not surprised, it's the sort of callous thing that fills his head most of the time."

"Let's just say, I'm beginning to understand the way he thinks, and it won't end well."

"Can I get you that drink now?" Emily offered.

"Please. Two white coffees with one sugar, thanks, Emily."

"What about the other officers, would they like one, too?"

Steve and Lee both smiled. "Not for us, we've not long had one," Steve said.

"I won't be long."

While Sara cleaned off her leather boots, she listened to the tractor going back and forth in the yard. "It makes quite a racket, doesn't it?"

Carla agreed. "I couldn't put up with that noise, day in, day out, but then, I'm out at work all day, so it wouldn't affect me."

"Yeah, but imagine if you were retired, listening to that din. It would drive you to distraction." Sara passed the hose to Carla who had slipped the bags off her boots.

"They're bloody ruined. Yours are leather, mine are suede."

"Don't be such a defeatist. Let's have a quick go. If not, I have a pair of trainers in the back of my car you can wear. They might stink a bit, but nothing in comparison to those."

"God, you're all heart."

"I know. Come on, let's crack on and get back to the station."

"What about the search?"

"I'll get Steve and Lee to join up with the other team. They should cover the estate in no time at all then. We can't hang around here, we have more important things to do."

"Such as?"

"I want to see what we can find out about Sanderson's and Fitt's connection. I think that's going to be the key to solving this case. The more I interact with Sanderson, the less I like him."

"I'm inclined to agree with you. What about Sanderson's son?"

"The jury is still out on that one."

CHAPTER 8

hey were halfway to the station when the call came in. Sara knew immediately that it was going to be bad news. She asked Carla to answer the phone and put it on speaker.

"DI Sara Ramsey, how can I help?"

"Sorry to trouble you, ma'am, it's Jeff. I have some devastating news about the lady reported missing, Alice Brown."

Sara indicated and pulled into a nearby parking place. "I'm listening, Jeff."

"Her body has been found down at the River Lugg at Lugwardine. Do you know the area I mean?"

"I think so, it's just off the main road, the A438, isn't it?"

"Yes, there's a lane opposite the Cock at Tupsley. I always use that track to get to the field when I take Rex there for a walk."

"I know it," Carla said. "Des and I sometimes go down there for a stroll when the weather is good."

"Okay, we've got it sorted. You might as well withdraw your guys from the estate. Has the pathologist been informed?"

"Yes, ma'am, she's on the way to the scene now with her team."

"Thanks, Jeff. We'll turn round and make our way over there now. This is a sad day for all concerned. Actually, scratch what I said about withdrawing your teams, can you ask Jason and Fiona to go back to the house to be with Emily instead?"

"Of course. Do you want them to break the news?"

Sara's long deliberation was brought to a halt with Carla jabbing her in the thigh.

"Do you?" Carla asked.

"I'm thinking. No, I think I should do it myself. Leave it with me for now. I want to check out the mother's injuries first. As soon as we've assessed the crime scene, we'll head back and have a chat with her. Maybe ask Jason and Fiona to sit tight outside the house in the meantime."

"Okay, whatever you want, ma'am. Good luck."

Sara ended the call and then thumped the steering wheel a couple of times until her hands hurt. "Shit, shit, shit! Why did she set foot outside that house?"

"She put the bin out! For Christ's sake, Sara, she's entitled to do that without having to think about her every move. Poor woman. Jesus, I can't imagine what this news is going to do to Emily. Both her parents gone in the blink of an eye. Killed, for what?"

"That's what we need to find out." Once the traffic had died down, Sara completed a three-point turn and drove to the crime scene under Carla's guidance.

"Yes, park the car here. We'll have to go on foot. I just hope it's not too muddy. Still, why should I care? My boots are already ruined anyway."

"Moan, moan, moan. I offered you a solution, but you refused to entertain it."

"Rightly so."

169

They entered the gate that led them into the local beauty spot for dog walkers and followed the path around the corner and into the next field which eventually passed by the river.

"Well, this is a hidden gem. I didn't even know this place existed," Sara said.

"I've been coming down here on Sundays for a jaunt for years. The team are hard at it." Carla pointed at a spot over to the right.

A marquee had been erected close to the river, and there were five or six techs milling around. Lorraine was there, issuing orders to her team.

"Damn, she's going to have a go at us for not wearing a suit."

"I'll pop back to the car and grab a couple, if you like?"

Sara smiled and handed her the keys. Then she continued along the grassy path to where the action was happening.

Lorraine glanced up and opened her mouth to speak.

Sara held her hand up. "Before you throw a wobbler, Carla's gone back to collect our suits. It's been a trying day, and it slipped our minds."

"It should be second nature for you by now, Inspector, when you show up at a crime scene."

A breathless Carla joined them and handed Sara a suit. They both slipped into them and the boot coverings that they should have considered using at the farm, then followed Lorraine into the tent to have a closer look at the victim.

Lorraine let the flap go behind them. "Female in her late fifties to early sixties. She's been dumped in the river."

"What injuries has she sustained? Is it the same MO or not?"

"I'd say partially. Maybe the killer got disturbed and couldn't complete his torturous intentions. This place is open and, according to one of my team, is used quite often during the day."

Sara stared at the victim, Alice Brown; there was no doubting it was her. "Just to give you a bit of background. This is the wife of victim two, Harry Brown. Her daughter reported her missing several hours ago after her mother put the bins out. We've had a couple of teams searching the area around the house most of the morning. The daughter is beside herself. Jesus, I've got no idea how she's going to react to this news."

"It's shocking," Lorraine agreed. "The killer obviously has an agenda. Haven't you got any leads yet?"

"We've got an inkling this is something to do with the farmer from a neighbouring farm. We paid him a visit earlier, asked if we could search the farmyard, looking for Alice, but found nothing. She was obviously already dead."

Lorraine frowned. "Did you tackle him about it?"

"I can't go tearing round there and accuse him outright. I had to make out that Alice was in a confused state and she might have wandered off."

"And what was his reaction?"

"He's a smarmy fucker. I could tell there was something going on, but let's say he disguises it well. Saying that, you need to do your part and find some evidence placing him at the scenes. Without that, we're up shit creek."

"Well, it's funny you should say that because she's been tied up. The rope must have come from somewhere. I know her husband was bound at the crime scene, but I believe that rope, a tow rope, probably came from the victim's car."

"So, how is this rope different?"

"It's thinner. Here, let me show you."

They crouched beside Alice's body. Her hands were tied behind her back by white rope that was slightly muddy.

"Now, this might be from the river," Lorraine said. "It's

171

quite shallow where she was found, and we don't know how far her body travelled before it ended up here, but I want to analyse it thoroughly, once we're back at the lab."

Sara got closer to the body and sniffed at the rope. "I don't think that's mud."

"What do you believe it is?" Lorraine said. She cocked an expectant eyebrow.

"We've had enough on our shoes this morning to know exactly what it is. Cow shit."

"Like I said, the fact she was found in the river needs to be taken into consideration, however, my first thoughts are that I'm inclined to agree with you."

Sara's thinking ramped up a notch. She scanned the area, unsure what she was hoping to find. "So, how was she killed?"

"She was strangled and stabbed a few times in the chest. The strangulation was most likely to have killed her. Then the killer began mutilating her body, similar to the way he did to the other victims. Her ears are missing, no telling where they are; it depends on where she was dumped in the river. It might have been here or possibly further upstream."

"Her mouth was sewn up, but her eyes left alone. Does that mean the killer ran out of time?" Sara asked.

Lorraine shrugged. "Anything is possible."

"Who found her?"

"The man and woman outside, over to the right. I asked them to hang around to speak with you. They're eager to get on their way, so make it quick."

"I'll chat to them now. This one is a tad perplexing, isn't it? I feel we're close but still too far away from knowing the truth to do anything about it. If that makes sense?"

"It does. Let's keep searching the area, see what we can find for you, while you have a chat with the witnesses."

"Sounds good to me." Sara struggled to get to her feet as

her suit had twisted, limiting her movement. "Damn thing, it's got a mind of its own."

Carla took a step forward to lend her a hand. "Either that or old age is setting in."

"Cheeky cow." Sara yanked her arm free from her partner's grasp, led the way out of the tent and crossed the field towards the anxious couple. "Hello, there. I'm DI Sara Ramsey, the officer in charge of the investigation. I'm sorry you were the ones who discovered the body. Thank you for calling nine-nine-nine."

"It was such a shock to find her... lying there, on the riverbank. If we hadn't decided to walk close by the river, I doubt if we would have seen her," the woman replied and started crying.

The man placed an arm around her shoulder and pulled her closer to him. "It's okay, Tania, the police will deal with her now."

"She's in safe hands," Sara confirmed. "Did you see anyone else when you arrived?"

The gentleman nodded. "The odd dog walker here and there. It's never really that busy down here, well, not during the week. Hang on, when we were getting out of the car there were two men rushing to get into an estate. I didn't notice if they had a dog or not so thought nothing of it at the time. But casting my mind back, their actions could be described as suspicious. Do you recall the ones I mean, Tania?"

"Yes. The ones who put their foot down when driving away?"

"Exactly. Most people take it easy leaving the area because the lane is quite narrow."

Sara's pulse raced. "I don't suppose you saw which direction they went in, did you?"

"I did. I thought it strange at the time... they went up the lane and then seconds later came tearing down the main road, along the A538, heading towards Worcester. At least I think it was them. It was the same colour car."

"I'm chancing my luck here, but I don't suppose you saw the number plate, did you?"

"Sadly not. Sorry. It all happened in a blur, and I didn't know I would be questioned by the police for discovering that poor woman's body over there, otherwise I would have taken more notice."

Sara smiled and waved her hand. "Don't worry. What about the men, would you be able to describe them?"

"Now you're testing me. What about you, Tania?"

"We can give it a try between us."

Carla withdrew her notebook and flicked it open to a new page.

"Going back to the car, any idea what make it was?" Sara asked.

"Possibly a silver BMW estate," the man said.

"Sorry, I didn't catch your name," Sara said.

"It's Colin Downey, and my wife is Tania Downey. The car was definitely silver as opposed to grey. I know that won't seem much difference to some folks, but it's the finer details you need, isn't it?"

"Yes, that's right. And the men you saw? What type of build did they have?"

"Both quite slender," his wife said. "One had quite messy brown hair, didn't look like it had been cut in a while, and the other man had hair at the sides but was balding on top. I used to be a hairdresser, in case you're wondering, so I tend to notice people's haircuts first and foremost."

"That's brilliant, very observant of you." *I'd call Sanderson's hair unkempt and in need of a cut. Things are looking up for us.*

"My wife is right. The man with the balding head wore jeans and a leather jacket. The other man, from what I saw of him before he got in the car, I believe he had on a type of dungarees or even overalls, but with a bib and brace. He also had a plaid shirt."

"Excellent. No jacket?" Sara asked, mentally visualising the outfit Sanderson had been wearing when they'd called at the farm barely an hour earlier.

"No. Can't say I noticed that."

"Anything else you can tell us?" Sara sensed there wasn't going to be, and she was eager to get on with the investigation.

"I don't think so. Maybe if anything comes to mind later we can get in touch."

Sara had to fight with her suit to find one of her cards in her jacket pocket. "Give me a call, day or night. We're going to need to take your details down. I'll send a uniformed officer round to take a statement in the next day or two, if that's okay with you?"

"Yes, that's fine," Mr Downey said. "We're both retired so at home most days. I'll give you my mobile number just in case."

"That'll be perfect. Thanks so much again for all your help today."

"I'd say it was a privilege but I'm not sure that's the right word for it. I hope she wasn't in the water long. It appals me to think she might have been in there all night."

"The pathologist will be able to tell the exact time of death, once she's performed the post-mortem. Take care of yourselves."

Sara walked back towards the crime scene and left Carla collecting the Downeys' details.

"How did you get on? You seem a little perplexed," Lorraine asked.

"We've got a description of two men who the couple saw leaving the area in a silver BMW estate."

"And?"

"And, I would say one of them sounds like it might be Sanderson, the farmer who is a person of interest."

"Then you have enough to take him in for questioning, don't you?"

"I'm still on the fence. The last thing I want to do is give him any indication that he's in the frame yet, not without further evidence at our disposal."

"What about the other man? Any idea who that might be?"

"Possibly. We have someone we're keen to have a chat with, but he's gone AWOL from work at present."

"Do you have his address?"

"Yes, that's going to be my next stop. I've had a few distractions that have got in the way, you know, like one or two, or even four murder scenes to attend over the past three, or is it four days? Sorry, I've lost count."

Lorraine rubbed her arm. "I wasn't having a go at you. Are you all right?"

Sara stared at her good friend for a while and shrugged. "You tell me."

Lorraine latched on to her elbow and guided her away from the others. "Do you want to talk?"

"About what? About dealing with four murders and not having any evidence to guide us or the fact I think my marriage is in the toilet?"

"What? That can't be right. You and Mark are as solid as a rock, you have been from day one. What's going on between you?"

"Nothing as far as I'm concerned. For some reason, he's shutting me out. He's away, staying with his parents. His mother is having an operation on a brain tumour and..."

"Stop right there. Then that's the issue, nothing to do with you. He's concerned about his mother. Brain surgery can be a tricky operation to tackle. He's a vet, he'll be aware of the risks involved."

"What are you saying? That I'm not? Of course I am. He's treating me like a stranger—no, as more of an inconvenience. He's never done that before, and I'm struggling to handle it. But I need to set that aside for now and concentrate on finding the two suspects before yet another body shows up."

"All right. Take a deep breath."

Carla joined them. "Everything okay here? Sara, what's going on?"

"She's having a panic attack," Lorraine said.

"What? How do we handle it?" Carla asked in a high-pitched tone.

"I *am not* having a panic attack. All I did was put my case across. You shouldn't have asked the question in the first place if you're going to overreact like this."

"Don't turn on me. It looked like you were struggling. Pardon me for being concerned." Lorraine stomped off in a huff.

Sara closed her eyes and shook her arms out to rid herself of the tension rippling through her body. "I don't need this. Can we get one thing straight...? I'm fine. I had a momentary lapse where I bared my soul, and this is the result. I'm one hundred percent fine and capable of conducting myself properly during an investigation. If I wasn't, you'd be the first to know."

Carla gave her a wary smile. "I'm glad to hear it. Right, what's the next step for us?"

"We need to break the news to Emily and then I think we should try and find Daniel Fitts, have a chat with him. Do me a favour, while I patch things up with Miss Frosty Knickers over there, can you see if you can source an image of Fitts via the internet?"

"Will do."

Sara went back to the crime scene and, at first, Lorraine gave her the cold shoulder while she dealt with the tech team.

After she'd finished dishing out her orders, she faced Sara and said, "I'm sorry if you thought I overstepped the mark, no pun intended."

"I didn't, and while I appreciate your concern, you need to allow me to get on with my life. At this moment in time, I can't do anything about the situation with Mark, not if he keeps blanking me. We both know what happens when people are pushed into doing something they don't want to do."

"I'll give you that one. I was just worried about you and wanted to offer some advice."

"Which I appreciate. Right, I need to keep my focus on the investigation. So, I'm going to pay the daughter a visit. I've got two officers with her right now. I might keep one at the house until…"

"You arrest the killer or killers?" Lorraine suggested.

"Yes. Crap, I don't think I've ever been in this situation before. I'm pretty sure that the farmer is involved but what if I'm wrong?"

"Go with your gut and worry about the consequences afterwards."

Sara laughed. "Cheers, and what if I end up losing my job?"

"You won't. Stop doubting yourself and get on with it, Sara. You've got this." Lorraine patted her on the shoulder.

"I've got this… yes, I have. Speak soon. In the meantime, keep searching for the evidence I need to bring down the killer or killers."

"I'm doing my best, I promise. We've got the rope. There might be other comparisons we can make between the crime scenes down the line. You're not the only one who has been snowed under this week... just saying."

"I know. I really appreciate what you and the team have achieved. Let's give it our all for the next few days, see where that leads us."

"That's a deal."

CHAPTER 9

$\mathcal{E}$mily was understandably in a terrible state after she heard the news. Sara was at a loss to know what to say to her. Fiona had agreed to stay with Emily for the foreseeable future. Sara had made her excuses to leave, not wishing the trail they were on to go cold. Outside, she asked Carla to request that Craig and Marissa join them at the estate.

"What are you planning?" Carla asked once she'd made the call and they were waiting for the others to join them.

"To visit Fitts. The image that showed up matches the description of the driver of the BMW. Hang on…" Sara fished out her phone from her pocket and rang the station. "Christine, I should have asked sooner, can you check for me what car Daniel Fitts drives?"

"Of course. Do you want me to call you back?"

"Yes, if you would."

"If he has a car registered to him of that description and it's parked outside the house when we get there, it's game over."

"And what about matey next door?"

Carla followed Sara along the side of the house to peer over the fence. All was quiet at the farm, not a soul in sight.

"That's the question. We're going to need to see how Fitts reacts during the interview."

"See if he cracks under the pressure?"

"Correct." A car drew up behind them. "Here's Craig and Marissa now."

They went back to the car to greet the other members of the team.

Sara's phone rang. "DI Sara Ramsey."

"It's Christine, boss. He drives a silver BMW estate."

"Brilliant. Can you give me the registration number? We're missing that information."

Christine gave the details which Sara repeated and Carla wrote down.

"Here we go then, folks, and this is the key point: Fitts' address is just up the road from here at Shucknall."

"It's sounding more and more likely all the time," Carla agreed, "and we're not too far from where Alice's body was found. We've got the farm next door and Fitts barely five minutes away. All three locations within striking distance of each other."

"They could have kidnapped Alice and killed her and both been back at their respective residences within thirty minutes of carrying out the deed," Sara suggested. "Yes, it's all slotting into place now. Let's see what Mr Fitts has to say for himself, if he's at home."

SARA HIGH-FIVED CARLA OUTSIDE FITTS' house when they saw the silver BMW estate sitting on the drive. "Looks like we're in luck."

Craig and Marissa pulled up in the space behind them, and the four of them approached the front door of the detached house. Sara smiled at the rest of her team and rang the bell. It was opened within seconds by Daniel Fitts. Sara recognised him not only from the photo on the council's website but also from the description the Downeys had given her.

"Yes. What do you want?" he asked, his gaze flitting between all of them.

Sara produced her ID. "Daniel Fitts? I'm DI Sara Ramsey. We're here hoping that you will be able to help us with our enquiries."

"It takes four detectives to come and visit me? What's this about?"

"Maybe it would be better if we came inside to speak with you, if it's convenient?"

"It's not. My wife is seriously ill and is resting in the lounge."

Sara glanced up at the frontage of the house. "What is this, a three- or four-bedroom house?"

"Four, why?"

"I'm sure you'll have more than one reception room at your disposal. Surely, we can use one of the other rooms, can't we?"

He heaved out a breath and held the door open. "If you insist. Take your shoes off and leave them outside, they look disgusting."

"Ah, yes, of course, we've had an interesting day that has led us into some unexpectedly filthy locations, shall we say?"

"I don't really care, just take them off."

He led them into the dining room which was separate from the kitchen. "Wait in here, I need to have a word with my wife, she'll be worried."

"Please do," Sara replied.

The four of them sat around the large oblong oak table, and Sara strained an ear to hear what was being said next door. After a few minutes, Fitts returned and sat opposite Sara.

"Is your wife all right?"

"She was diagnosed with MS about three months ago and has recently taken a turn for the worst."

"I'm sorry to hear that. It must be hard, you having an important job with the council and your wife needing assistance every day."

"We usually have a carer during the week, but she rang in sick a couple of days ago. I had little option other than to take time off."

"Yes, we were told you had a family emergency on your hands when we tried to speak to you at the office."

"You rang my office? May I ask why?"

"To speak with you regarding an investigation we're working on."

"Are you going to continue going around in circles or are you going to tell me what you're talking about, Inspector? I'm pushed for time. My wife can't be trusted to be alone for long, she's prone to falling over a lot."

"Okay, I can get to the point, with pleasure. We've been told by a few of the residents from the new housing estate down in Withington that they have contacted you to make a formal complaint about the farm next door. I believe it's called Low Rise Farm, is that correct?"

"It is."

"Can you tell us what the outcome of those complaints were?"

"As I keep telling the residents, farms are regarded as complex entities and work under different restrictions to the norm."

Sara frowned. "I'm sorry, I don't understand."

"We've received several noise pollution complaints. The usual guideline is that people aren't allowed to make excessive noise outside the hours of eleven in the evening and seven in the morning, but those restrictions don't apply to farms because of the nature of their business at different times of the year."

"That's news to me," Sara stated. "Why?"

Fitts shrugged. "I don't make the rules up."

"No, but you're there as an Environmental Health Officer to enforce them."

"You're not listening to me, Inspector. As I've told the residents, time and time again I might add, my hands are tied."

"Ludicrous, absolutely ridiculous. So, the residents have to put up with the noise pollution and there's not a sodding thing anyone can do about it?"

"Correct. My team and I monitor all the complaints that come in. If they become excessive then we would need to reassess the situation."

"So there is something you can do?"

"Not really. All we can do is have a word with the farmer, ask him to be more considerate to the people living around him."

"And have you done that?" Sara asked.

"Yes. Every time a complaint comes in."

"And yet things have escalated over time, to the extent that some of the residents had to move house. And you think that's acceptable?"

"I told you, I don't make the rules. Excuse me, I need to check on my wife. Can I get you a drink?"

"Go ahead. I can make the drinks for you, if you'll allow me to?"

"Fine. Everything is in the kitchen on the side, and the milk is in the fridge."

They parted at the doorway, and Sara filled the kettle in the large kitchen. She peered out of the bi-fold doors that led onto the garden at the rear that was beautifully maintained. She returned to prepare the drinks, and Carla joined her a few minutes later.

"He's taking his time," Carla whispered.

"I haven't got a clue how bad people with MS can get. I'll make the drinks and then check on them, see if I can lend a hand."

Carla helped Sara carry the drinks into the dining room, and then Sara craned her neck from the doorway.

"I can't hear them. I'll be right back." She made her way up the hallway, and a shaft of light caught her attention. *Shit! The front door is bloody open.* She knocked gently on the lounge door and eased it open, only to find a woman sleeping on the couch. Fitts was nowhere to be seen. She closed the door again and ran back to the dining room.

"He's done one. The front door is open."

The four of them dashed out of the house. Sara deliberated whether she should stay with Mrs Fitts or not, but her welfare hadn't been at the top of her husband's agenda, had it? So why should she consider it?

"Craig, ring the station. Get backup out here. Put an alert out on his car, too."

Sara thumped her thigh. "I'm going to see if one of the neighbours will sit with the wife for a while."

"Bloody hell, what a bastard to desert his wife like this," Carla said.

"Yep, I'm not about to disagree with you. Vile man." Sara finished putting on her shoes and opened the gate to the neighbour's house.

A woman in her early forties opened the door a smidgen and frowned. "Can I help you?"

Sara held up her warrant card and introduced herself. "I'm sorry to trouble you. Is there any possibility you can sit with the lady next door for a little while?"

"What? Why would I want to do that? We don't get along, never have done, not since they moved in. He thinks he's better than the rest of us, is always looking down his nose at us."

"Damn, okay. What about the other neighbour?"

"Nope, I wouldn't have thought Elaine would be willing to help out either. What's going on?"

"The lady is ill, and she needs someone to be there with her."

"Where's he gone? I saw him drive off in a rush a few minutes ago."

"You did? Which direction did he go in?"

"To the left, towards Worcester. Couldn't he have stuck around and looked after his wife?"

"No. I'm sorry, I don't have time to stand around chatting, I have to go after the husband. Please, please won't you reconsider and be a good neighbour?"

"I've always been good to them, not that it has got me very far. All right, let me grab my keys and put some shoes on."

"Thank you, I really do appreciate you helping us out like this."

The woman grunted and closed the inner door to the house. Sara gave Carla the thumbs-up and mouthed, "He's heading towards Worcester, let the station know."

Carla withdrew her phone from her pocket and made the call.

The woman reappeared and closed the door behind her. "This is against my better judgement, but it's not in me to be mean to someone in need. I'm only doing it because you said the wife is ill. Have they broken the law in some way?"

"Not as far as we know. We showed up to ask Mr Fitts some questions, and he decided to take off."

"Ha, well, he wouldn't have done that if he wasn't guilty, would he?"

"I suppose not. Sorry, what's your name?"

"Jill Meadows. I can only spare thirty minutes because I've arranged to pick up my daughter."

"We should be back by then."

"Blimey, there's four of you and you couldn't spare someone to sit with her? That seems strange to me. Even stranger than him taking off like that."

"Thanks again. We'll be back soon, I promise." Sara saw Jill into the house and, with her conscience now clear, she joined the others. "Right, the neighbour seems to think he's en route to Worcester. He can't be that far ahead of us. So, we use the blues and twos and don't hold back until we've caught up with the bastard. Carla and Marissa, you're going to need to keep your eyes open while Craig and I do the driving. Let's go."

FIFTEEN MINUTES LATER, Sara's heart sank faster and faster with their lack of achievement until the silver BMW came into view. It was caught up in traffic about ten cars ahead of them. With her siren blaring, she flew past the other cars and pulled up alongside a panic-stricken Fitts.

Carla lowered her window, and Sara shouted, "Switch your engine off, you're nicked."

Craig had driven onto the pavement on the other side and successfully blocked Fitts in.

Fitts slammed his fists onto his steering wheel. Sara got out of her car to the sound of horns blasting, the other drivers letting her know how impatient they were to get moving again. She opened Daniel's car door and slapped a pair of cuffs on his wrists and ordered him to get in the back seat of her vehicle.

"You can't do this. I've done nothing wrong."

"Why run? All you've done is prove you're guilty in the eyes of the law." Sara signalled for the cars behind them to pull out and drive around them. "Craig, can you shift the car off the road so it's not causing an obstruction? We'll head back to the station."

"You can't make me go with you. What about my wife?"

"Wow, I've heard it all now. Funny that, you weren't thinking about your wife when you tried to escape."

"But…"

"Your neighbour, Jill, has agreed to sit with her until other arrangements can be made."

"I don't want that woman anywhere near her. Let me go home, check she's okay and allow me to call someone else to come and sit with her."

"You're not going home. You can make a call when we get to the station."

"But she needs me," he whined.

Sara didn't think his comment was worthy of a reply, not after he'd absconded without giving his wife a second thought. She opened the back door of her car and nudged him to get in.

"But this isn't right, I've done nothing wrong."

"Get in or I'll force you in, the choice is yours."

He finally relented, and Sara turned to the drivers still stuck behind and waved an apology. She drove on and turned up an alley about half a mile up the road. A gap in the traffic allowed her to reverse onto the main road, and she headed back towards Hereford. They passed Craig and Marissa on the way, and she gestured for them to turn around.

. . .

SARA RANG AHEAD to arrange for the interview room to be prepared for their arrival. Jeff was happy to oblige. Carla and a uniformed officer accompanied Fitts down the corridor.

Sara paused to speak to the desk sergeant and explained the situation to him. "Trouble is, until he starts speaking, we can't bring Sanderson in."

"That's a tough one, ma'am. Do you want me to send a couple of members of my team out there? They can keep the farm under surveillance and pounce on the farmer if he tries to escape if he gets wind of Fitts being here."

"Good idea. I get the impression he's not going to take long to crack."

The main door opened behind them, and the duty solicitor joined them.

"Hello, Miss Connell, nice of you to join us," Sara said. "I'll show you to the interview room. Your client is in there already."

"Hello, Inspector. That sounds great. What's he been arrested for?"

"He hasn't been, yet. We've brought him in to help us with our enquiries."

"Did he come willingly?"

"That's where the problem lies. He absconded from the property, leaving his very ill wife unattended."

"I see. Sounds like a right charmer, not that I'm judging."

"You'll soon see for yourself. Between you and me, we have reason to believe he's in cahoots with another man and they've killed four people this week. We just need him to start singing, and bingo."

"Well, you know I can't help you there. All I can do is wish you luck, but thanks for giving me the heads-up. Are you going to tell me if you have any evidence that places my client at any of the murder scenes?"

Sara tapped the side of her nose. "Ah, sorry, that's privileged information."

They both laughed.

Sara led the way down the corridor. "We'll give you ten minutes. Sergeant Jameson, if you'd like to join me."

Carla left the room, and together they climbed the stairs to join the rest of the team. Craig and Marissa arrived not long after. Carla made them all a drink.

"Well, that was a close one," Sara said. "Good job, guys. Now the real work begins, trying to get the information out of him. We need to bury the pair of them. Jeff has a team en route to the farm. They'll keep the farmer under surveillance until we give them further instructions."

FIFTEEN MINUTES LATER, Sara and Carla entered Interview Room One.

"Can I get anyone a drink before we start?" Sara asked.

"No, thank you, Inspector," Miss Connell said, "we're both eager to get on with the proceedings."

"Yes, my wife needs me," Fitts added, his gaze fixed on his clenched hands.

"Very well. Sergeant, if you can say the necessary for the tape to get the interview underway."

Carla hit the play button on the machine.

"My first question, Mr Fitts, is why you felt it necessary to abscond from an interview we were holding at your home earlier."

"I… felt under pressure, intimidated with four of you there. I needed to get away to clear my head."

"Ah, I see. Why didn't you just say that and ask to take a break in the garden? Why leave the house, where your sick wife was, and take off?"

"I don't know, I regret that now."

"You regret it, why? Because you got caught? Or because guilt has set in regarding your wife's welfare?"

"Whatever."

"What's your connection with Robert Sanderson?"

His gaze met hers. "There isn't one."

"Isn't there? We believe differently. It would be in your best interests if you revealed all. Do that, and you could be back home with your wife within the next hour or so."

He swiftly turned to look at his solicitor. She kept her head down, studying her notes.

"I... no, this is some kind of trick. You're using my wife's illness to your advantage."

"Am I? I don't think I am. What's your connection with Robert Sanderson?"

"I haven't got one. Talking of my wife, I don't want that nosey neighbour anywhere near her."

"Ah, yes," Miss Connell said, "my client mentioned that you had arranged for a neighbour to sit with his wife. He's uncomfortable about the situation and would like to rectify it as quickly as possible."

"Okay, I'll give him permission to make the necessary arrangements for someone to replace the neighbour."

"Good," Fitts said. "I can call my sister."

Sara paused the recording and allowed Fitts to make the call from his mobile.

"Vicky, yeah, it's me. I'm in trouble and need your help... Listen and I'll tell you... I'm at the police station, helping the police with their enquiries. One of our neighbours is sitting with Helen, someone I can't abide. Is there any chance you can go over to the house and sit with her...? I don't know how long I'm going to be... No, the usual carer is off sick... I *had* taken time off work to be with her. Look, can you go over there or not...? That's brilliant, thanks so much. I'll make it up to you one day."

He ended the call and slid his mobile to the side of the table.

"See, there are people willing to help when you need it," Sara said. "Shall we continue?"

He shrugged.

Carla started the recording once more.

"This is the third time I'm asking this question, Mr Fitts," Sara said. "What's your connection with Robert Sanderson, the farmer at Low Rise Farm in Withington?"

"I've dealt with him a few times in my role as an Environmental Health Officer."

"Thank you. May I ask why?"

"You know why, because of the complaints my department has received regarding the noise coming from the farm."

"And would you say your friendship has grown during the time you've known him?"

"What kind of question is that?"

"An important one. Please answer it truthfully."

"I suppose the answer is yes."

Sara nodded. "Over time, how has that friendship manifested?"

He fell silent and clenched his hands together tightly until his knuckles turned white.

"Why don't I fill in the blanks for you?" Sara said. "In the past week, four people have been killed in Hereford. They have one significant connection."

He lifted his head, and his eyes narrowed. "What the fuck does this have to do with me?"

"I'm coming to that. The connection I'm talking about is the newbuild estate situated in Withington, adjacent to Robert Sanderson's farm. Are you keeping up with me?"

"Yes. I still don't know what any of this has to do with me."

"I'm coming to that part. The victims, over the past few years, have raised serious complaints with the Environmental Health, and you're the officer who has dealt with their grievances."

He shrugged. "As my role of chief EH officer, I deal with most of the complaints that come into our office, in one way or another, depending on the severity of the matter in hand."

"I see, thank you for clarifying that point. Perhaps you can tell us where you were today at around eleven this morning?"

"Caring for my wife, who is seriously ill with MS."

"Okay, are you sure you haven't left her side today?"

"I'm sure." His gaze drifted off to the left.

It was something Sara was always on the lookout for during an interview. Invariably, all liars did it at one time or another.

"Ah, you see, we have it on good authority that you were seen getting into your silver BMW with another man, whom we believe to be Robert Sanderson."

"What? No way, you're mistaken. I haven't left the house. You're trying to stitch me up here."

"I assure you, we're not. We have two very reliable witnesses who have given us a statement placing you and Robert Sanderson at the scene of a murder." Sara knew she was guilty of stretching the truth, but it was a necessary ploy to get a reaction out of the suspect. "ANPR is being looked at as we speak, and it will show whether you left the house or not."

He stood and tipped his chair back then slammed his fists on the table. "I'm innocent. I didn't do anything. You can't do this to me."

The uniformed officer stepped forward and urged Fitts to sit down. The officer righted the chair, and Fitts dropped into it.

"That was quite an emotional reaction you gave there, Mr Fitts. Can you tell us why?"

"Because I haven't done anything wrong."

"Do you have anything to do with the murders?"

He sat there, staring at her.

She could sense the cogs turning in his mind. "Your silence is deafening. How did your involvement with Sanderson begin? What's really going on between you? Apart from killing innocent people who have complained about the farm."

His gaze dipped to the table, and he wrung his hands. "I didn't want any of this."

"Any of what? Killing four innocent people?"

"He had me over a barrel, and I couldn't see any way out of the fix I was in. He forced me to take part."

"Take part? In the murders?" Sara pushed.

"Yes."

There it was, his confession, all wrapped up in a neat bow. Carla nudged her knee under the table.

"Now that you've admitted to being involved in the murders, why don't you tell us how this has come about?"

"It was Sanderson's fault. Well, he caught me at my lowest ebb. My wife hasn't been well for a while. It's only recently the doctors have been able to give her a proper diagnosis. I needed to go private for some treatment for her, and we were short of funds. Sanderson had been on at me for ages, asking me who the people who had complained about him were. He was desperate to obtain the names and…"

"And he offered you money in exchange for their details?" Sara filled in for him.

"Yes. At first, I didn't see a problem telling him. But then he kept hassling me, wanting more and more information. He was on the brink of losing it, under pressure from the people he does business with."

"Wait, what business? Selling the cows?"

He shook his head. "There's more going on at that farm than you think, which is why he was livid when the police kept showing up out of the blue. At the end of his tether, he told me he was going to do away with the people who had complained about him. It was the only way he could see to stop the police turning up at the farm. I told him he was nuts. He was furious, said that I had to be his accomplice."

Sara flipped her notebook open and jotted down a message to Carla. *Tell Jeff to arrest Robert Sanderson.* Sara announced for the recording that Carla had left the room.

Fitts frowned in confusion.

Sara ignored his unspoken question. "Go on. Wait, is Sanderson's son involved in the crimes?"

"No, he was desperate to keep the lad out of it, that's why he wanted muggins here to do the dirty work for him."

"It was you who followed Sanderson out to Lower Lyde, where Harry Brown was killed, then you dropped him back to the college to pick up his car, didn't you?"

"Yes. I had to. You've got to believe me. He's a nasty fucker. I took money from him and that was it. He had me in his clutches and refused to let go."

"Okay. You mentioned there was more going on at the farm than we know, such as?"

"Drugs. He makes and stores drugs in the outbuildings at the back of his land. The cows are a sideline. He loses money raising them for market to sell into the meat trade, but they're an excellent front for his other business."

"Why kill Alice this morning? Who abducted her outside her house?"

His head lowered. "That was me. Sanderson rang me, told me she was next on the list to die, and he was waiting for the opportunity. That came today. She was out front tending to her garden most of the morning and then she put the bins out. Sanderson kept ringing me, telling me to get a move on, but my wife was really ill and I couldn't leave her. He pressured me so much I had to give Helen some sleeping tablets. That's why she was still asleep when you called at the house and why I knew she would be safe if I made a run for it. I wasn't thinking straight. I know I put both of us in jeopardy, but we were desperate and needed the money."

"So you got into bed with the devil, right?"

Carla came back and nodded at Sara.

"For the recording, DS Jameson has returned to the room. What about the other murders? What can you tell me about them? Were you present when the victims were killed?"

"Yes. I was there. He *forced* me to be there. To watch them take their last breaths. It was done on purpose, so I understood what was likely to happen to me and my wife if I opened my mouth and reported the crimes to the police. I haven't slept a wink since the first murder. I had to call in sick, there's no way I could've handled being at work this week. He's insane. A greedy bastard who doesn't care about anyone but himself. I wish I'd never got involved with him."

"By then it was too late to back out?"

"Yes. There have been occasions when I've been desperate enough to want to end it all, but then who would look after my wife? No one, they're all selfish. You heard how much I had to plead with Vicky to go and sit with her. No one offers to stay with Helen while I go shopping or have an urgent appointment after the carer has finished for the day. My family never come near me because they can't stand seeing Helen the way she is, and yet I have to watch her getting worse by the hour most days. Hence my involvement with Sanderson. I just wanted the best for my wife. Treatment that is not available on the NHS."

"Meaning?"

"There's a place in America that has been doing major

research with MS patients. That was my next step, to get my hands on enough money to take her there, see if they could cure her once and for all."

Sara shook her head. "Couldn't you have created a GoFundMe account instead? Why get caught up with Sanderson and get involved with the murders of four innocent people? Your logic is beyond me. To save one life, you thought it was okay to end four lives into the bargain. Where would it have ended if you hadn't got caught?"

He ran a hand through his hair. "I don't know, and yes, that's the honest answer. I love my wife dearly and will clearly do anything for her. To have her back again, the way she was, that's all we've ever wanted."

"And now all that will be taken away from you. You're going to spend decades behind bars, and your wife will spend the rest of her life without you by her side, probably in a council-run care home."

He broke down in tears. Sara felt numb. She had no feelings either way for the man who had sat back and refused to step in to save the lives of the four victims.

"I think my client needs to take a break now, Inspector," Miss Connell said.

"I agree. We'll make you comfortable in a cell and continue the interview in a few hours, if you're agreeable to that, Miss Connell."

"Of course."

Carla ended the recording, and the officer whisked Fitts out of the room. Sara and Carla escorted Miss Connell back to the reception area. They were halfway up the corridor when shouting broke out. Sara tore down the corridor area to find Sanderson being restrained by two officers.

Sara pushed Fitts towards the cells. "Get him locked up. Now."

The officer who had accompanied Fitts from the interview room looked sheepish. "Sorry, ma'am. I was guilty of taking my eye off the ball. Had no idea the other bloke was in there."

"I don't want to hear your excuses, just get him out of here."

"If you've opened that mouth of yours, Fitts, I'll fucking have you for it," Sanderson shouted.

"Showing your true colours, are we, Sanderson?" Sara asked.

"Screw you, bitch. You should have kept your nose out. You have no idea who you're dealing with."

"Is that a threat you've just made in public, Mr Sanderson?"

"Fuck off, wench. You'll get what's coming to you. I'll make sure you'll be forever looking over your shoulder until the day you die."

"People like you don't scare me, Sanderson. I feel sorry for you because that's all you've got now, isn't it? The ability to mouth off, and even that is going to go against you in court."

Sara smiled, and Sanderson spat at her. Luckily, Sara was out of range.

"A piss-poor shot. You can't even get that right. Sergeant, throw him in a cell. I'll deal with him when I'm ready." Sara turned on her heel and marched up the stairs to the incident room where she let out a relieved breath.

Carla laughed and patted her on the back. "Bravo. That was a masterclass in dealing with scumbag criminals."

"You mean scumbag murderers. I have a couple of calls to make. I need to tell Emily and Gail we've arrested the bastards."

. . .

EMILY WAS FILLED with mixed emotions when Sara shared the news of the arrests, but she did say how grateful she was to Sara and her team for giving the investigation their all and for arresting the perpetrators early, so yet more families didn't have to go through the same distress as she was going through.

Then Sara updated Gail Smith. The woman broke down straight away. So much so that Sara felt guilty and even regretted sharing the news over the phone instead of going to see her in person. Gail had taken the news badly and kept repeating, "Why did they target my family?" When Sara revealed the motive behind the killings, Gail fell silent. Every part of Sara ached for the woman's loss. The lives of her husband and son had been needlessly lost because they'd stuck up for themselves and their neighbours' rights to have a peaceful life. What a waste!

PHONING Emily and Gail had put Sara in the right frame of mind to deal with Robert Sanderson. She was ready.

Sanderson glared at Sara during Carla's speech to begin the interview.

Another duty solicitor was in attendance. This time Ian Bristow was sitting alongside his client.

Sara smiled at Sanderson. "Okay, Robert, let's not beat around the bush here. After our conversation with Daniel Fitts in which he revealed his involvement in the murders of Joshua and Allan Smith and Harry and Alice Brown, he told us that you hatched the plan to take revenge on the victims. I have one question for you: why?"

He gave a cheesy grin and leaned forward to say, "No comment."

"I had a feeling you would go down that route, not that it matters, not when we have Fitts' full confession to hand. I'll also be bringing your son in for questioning once I've concluded this interview."

He slammed his hand on the table. "Leave Bobby out of it. He had nothing to do with the murders. I only killed those fuckers to protect his future."

"Ah, so you admit to committing the murders of the four innocent victims?"

He shrugged, and his gaze dropped for the first time during the interview.

"Why get involved with drugs? How long has that been going on?" Sara pushed, determined to get to the truth now that she had him by the short and curlies.

"No comment."

"We will get to the bottom of this. Once word gets around that you've been arrested, do you truly believe whoever you're working with won't set their sights on Bobby?"

"I want him left out of it. You need to protect him."

Sara wagged her finger. "Oh no, we won't be able to intervene there. The only time the police offer assistance is if someone is willing to work with us. That's down to you. If you insist on answering 'no comment' to my questions, let's face it, you're not doing either yourself or your son any favours, are you?"

His head rose, and his gaze latched on to hers once more. "All right, I'll give you names, but only once my son has been placed somewhere safe."

"I can run that past my DCI, see if she agrees."

"Do it, now. My son is in grave danger."

Sara tutted and rose from her seat. For the recording, Carla announced that she was leaving the room, and then Sara made the call to DCI Price who had no hesitation in agreeing to the terms with one proviso: that Sanderson told them everything and left nothing out.

Returning to the room, and once the recording had

started again, Sara relayed the message from DCI Price. "We want names, *all of them*, involved in the drug side of your business."

"I'll give them after my son has been picked up and taken to the safe house."

"Nope, you're in no position to make demands. I'm telling you what will happen: you give us all the names of your contacts, and I'll hold up my end of the bargain and offer your son protection. The choice, as they say, is yours."

It took a few moments of Sanderson intently glaring at Sara before he finally broke down and divulged the information. Sara called a halt to the interview and instructed the constable to escort Sanderson back to his cell.

"What about Bobby? You promised," he shouted from the doorway.

"Unlike some people, I never go back on my word. Bobby will be picked up and taken to a safe house once I have the information corroborated by the drug squad."

"What? That wasn't what you said at all."

"It was. You can't expect me to trust the information you've given me without checking it out first. It won't take long. You have my word that Bobby will be picked up before the day is over. That's the best I can do in the circumstances."

He left the room ranting and shouting expletive after expletive.

They accompanied the solicitor back to the reception area, and then Sara and Carla climbed the stairs to the incident room.

"There's just no pleasing some folks, is there?" Sara grumbled.

"He thought he had you over a barrel. Tosser. What about the thirty grand in Joshua's account?"

"I suppose it'll come to light eventually. If I were to hazard a guess, I wouldn't put it past Sanderson to have tried to have paid him off. Maybe Joshua agreed to get the neighbours to stop ringing the police and, when he failed to do it, perhaps that's when the red mist descended and, Sanderson went on the killing spree."

"Seems logical."

The next couple of hours consisted of the team doubling their efforts to get all the paperwork completed. Sara passed on the details she'd been given to Ray Timmings in the drug squad, who she had worked with a few times in the past. He told her his team had been monitoring the farm for a while and were closing in on Sanderson and his activities. When Sara told him about the four murders the suspect had committed that week, he wasn't surprised in the slightest.

After their shift, Sara and her team stopped at the pub for a celebratory drink, even though Sara's heart wasn't in it. To her surprise, DCI Price joined them.

"I thought you'd be here," Carol Price said after buying a round of drinks for the team.

"Am I that predictable?" Sara asked.

Carol cocked an eyebrow. "You can be at times."

As the evening drew to a close, Carol said, "Right, the real reason I hunted you down this evening is to order you to take some time off."

Sara opened her mouth ready to object.

"Don't even go there. Your family need you."

Sara tipped her head back and whispered, "The truth is, I don't think they do."

"Nonsense. Your husband has been testing you."

Her words struck a chord. "You really think that?"

"Absolutely. He wants to see how far you're prepared to put your loyalty for the job before your relationship and family."

"Bugger. I didn't even stop to consider that. Shit. Have I left it too late?"

Carol shrugged. "There's only one way to find out. Go home, pack a bag, get a good night's sleep, and then hit the road first thing in the morning. Carla and the rest of the team can handle things for a few days, can't you, Carla?"

"Of course."

"No, I can't go, we're still a man down. What about Barry?"

"I took the liberty of calling him. He assured me that everything is now fine at home, and he had every intention of coming back to work on Monday and, as it is the team's weekend off, it has worked out well, hasn't it?"

"Okay, if you put it like that, I'll take the time off."

"Take as long as you need," Carol said. She downed the rest of her drink and left the pub, her mission accomplished.

"Are you all right?" Carla whispered in Sara's ear.

"Shell-shocked, if you must know. I'm going to head home."

Carla hugged her. "Good luck. Remember what Price said."

"I will, thanks. I'll ring you over the weekend."

"I'd be upset if you didn't."

EPILOGUE

*W*ith Misty being cared for by her neighbours, at ten forty-five the following morning, Sara parked her car a few doors down from Mark's parents' house. She inhaled and exhaled a couple of steadying breaths and then made her way towards the house.

She rang the bell and waited.

The door opened seconds later, and Mark stood there. "What the...?"

"Hello. I thought I'd surprise you." Sara took a step towards him.

Mark flinched, and his eyes teared up.

"Mark, what's going on? Aren't you pleased to see me?"

"Of course I am." He held out his hand and pulled her close. "I've missed you so much. I thought I had lost you."

Sara kissed him on the cheek and hugged him. His body trembled against hers. "You'd never lose me. What's going on?"

"It's Mum, she's taken a turn for the worst, and they've decided to operate again to relieve the pressure on her brain."

"Oh shit. I'm so sorry. Where's your father?"

"He's at the hospital. He told me to come home. He insisted he wanted to stay there during the operation. I was exhausted. I've barely slept a wink since I got here. I said I would take Rascal for a long walk before I go back to the hospital."

"Can I come with you?"

"Dad would love that."

He showed her into the house, and Rascal, the Border terrier, barked and then greeted her excitedly.

"In your basket, boy. Come on, behave now," Mark said.

"He's fine, don't worry. How are you holding up?" Sara asked.

Mark made them both a cup of coffee, and they sat at the table, holding hands. She was confident she had made the right decision by coming. "I'm okay."

"How long is the operation expected to take?"

"Two hours. Mum was fading fast yesterday. Dad and I were both really concerned about her."

"And what prognosis has the doctor given?"

"He hasn't. It's Dad I'm worried about. If we lose Mum, it's going to hit him hard. She's everything to him."

"That's why we need to think positively. We need to remain strong and be there for him, Mark."

"I know. Sara, there's something I need to tell you... something I've been keeping from you for a few months."

Oh God, here it comes. He's got someone else and wants a divorce. She swallowed down the bile that erupted in her throat and said, "Go on."

He gripped her hand tighter, confusing her further. "Mum's not the only one who is ill."

"What? Who else, your father?"

"No, me."

"You're not. How ill?" Her vision misted, and her throat closed over.

"I found a lump."

"Where?" Her heart pounded, and she gripped his hand tighter still.

"My left testicle."

She hugged him. Mark rested his head on her shoulder and sobbed.

"We'll get through this, together. We all will. I love you, Mark."

"Will we? I love you, Sara. Forgive me for trying to push you away. I thought I was doing the right thing."

She kissed him, silencing his doubts.

THE END

THANK you for reading Revenge Streak, Sara and Carla's next adventure can be found here Seeking Retribution.

HAVE you read any of my fast paced other crime thrillers yet? Why not try the first book in the award-winning Justice series Cruel Justice here.

OR THE FIRST book in the spin-off Justice Again series, Gone In Seconds.

WHY NOT TRY the first book in the DI Sam Cobbs series, set in the beautiful Lake District, To Die For.

· · ·

PERHAPS YOU'D PREFER to try one of my other police procedural series, the DI Kayli Bright series which begins with <u>The Missing Children.</u>

OR MAYBE YOU'D enjoy the DI Sally Parker series set in Norfolk, <u>Wrong Place.</u>

OR MY GRITTY police procedural starring DI Nelson set in Manchester, <u>Torn Apart.</u>

OR MAYBE YOU'D like to try one of my successful psychological thrillers <u>She's Gone</u>, <u>I KNOW THE TRUTH</u> or <u>Shattered Lives.</u>

KEEP IN TOUCH WITH M A COMLEY

Pick up a FREE novella by signing up to my newsletter today.
https://BookHip.com/WBRTGW

BookBub
www.bookbub.com/authors/m-a-comley

Blog

http://melcomley.blogspot.com

Why not join my special Facebook group to take part in monthly giveaways.

Readers' Group

Printed in Great Britain
by Amazon

37023342R00126